**"I didn't c
you tro**

"I just don't want any part of the media hype surrounding you and your son, Eli," Maggie said. Kane almost believed her.

Almost believed her, but didn't.

Kane dealt with secrets every day. He knew when a person was hiding something.

Right now, he had no choice but to let her keep her secrets, but Kane had no intention of letting Maggie suffer because of the part she'd played in bringing Eli home.

"Okay."

"What do you mean, 'okay'?"

"You've got a right to your privacy. Whatever your secrets are, I'm not going to try to uncover them. But if you're in trouble because of what you've done for my family, I'll do whatever it takes to help."

"Are you in trouble, Ms. Tennyson?" Eli asked. Kane could have kicked himself for giving his son more to be anxious about.

He wanted to find out what was really going on, but doing so in front of Eli wasn't smart. Kane would bide his time, wait until he had a chance to speak to Maggie alone, and then he'd try to get to the bottom of things....

Books by Shirlee McCoy

Love Inspired Suspense

Die Before Nightfall
Even in the Darkness
When Silence Falls
Little Girl Lost
Valley of Shadows
Stranger in the Shadows
Missing Persons
Lakeview Protector
*The Guardian's Mission
*The Protector's Promise
Cold Case Murder
*The Defender's Duty
**Running for Cover
Deadly Vows
**Running Scared

*The Sinclair Brothers
**Heroes for Hire

Steeple Hill

Still Waters

SHIRLEE McCOY

has always loved making up stories. As a child, she daydreamed elaborate tales in which she was the heroine— gutsy, strong and invincible. Though she soon grew out of her superhero fantasies, her love for storytelling never diminished. She knew early that she wanted to write inspirational fiction, and began writing her first novel when she was a teenager. Still, it wasn't until her third son was born that she truly began pursuing her dream of being published. Three years later she sold her first book. Now a busy mother of five, Shirlee is a homeschool mom by day and an inspirational author by night. She and her husband and children live in Washington and share their house with a dog, two cats and a bird. You can visit her Web site at www.shirleemccoy.com, or e-mail her at shirlee@shirleemccoy.com.

Shirlee McCoy

RUNNING SCARED

Steeple
Hill®

Published by Steeple Hill Books™

STEEPLE HILL BOOKS

Steeple
Hill®

Recycling programs
for this product may
not exist in your area.

ISBN-13: 978-0-373-44400-7

RUNNING SCARED

www.SteepleHill.com

Printed in U.S.A.

For you have delivered me from death and my feet from stumbling, that I may walk before God in the light of life.

—*Psalms* 56:13

To my daughter's other family. May God bless you abundantly for the love you give to the children whose lives you touch.

And to my parents, Edward and Shirley Porter. You have taught me the two most important lessons of all—the value of faith and the value of family. Thank you.

ONE

The wind howled, throwing ice and rain against the windows and roof of Maggie Tennyson's attic apartment. She shivered, grabbing a thick flannel shirt and tossing it over her fitted T-shirt. It was a good night to stay inside, snuggled up in front of a glowing fire, reading a book, drinking cocoa, maybe even watching a movie.

Too bad that wasn't an option.

She grabbed her duffel bag and the satchel that contained the day's ungraded tests, slipped into her coat and hurried out the door and down a flight of stairs that led to the Victorian bungalow's spacious foyer. The tinny sound of the television drifted from the living room, its flickering blue light splashing across the hardwood floor as Maggie tiptoed past the open door.

The old wood floor creaked beneath her feet, and she hurried forward, turning the doorknob and pulling open the front door. Cold air blew in, carrying icy winter rain and the sharp, crisp scent of pine needles.

"Maggie Mae? Where in the world are you going?" Edith Lancaster peered out of the living room, her eyes flashing with curiosity.

"Out to the house," Maggie responded, closing the door and turning to face her landlady. She didn't have time for explanations and conversation, but trying to dodge either would be like waving a red flag at a bull. Better to give Edith a few answers inside the house than to be followed out into the rain and waylaid on the front porch where anyone could see her.

"On a night like tonight? Are you sure that's a good idea?" Edith stepped into the foyer, her sharp brown eyes taking in everything. The bulging duffel. The satchel. Maggie's faded jeans and wool coat, her gloves and hat.

"It's a long weekend. I figure I can get quite a bit done on the house over the next four days." Could Edith hear the slight trembling of Maggie's voice? Could she hear the fear in it?

"Maybe, but I still don't think going out to the Miller monstrosity on a night like tonight is a good idea."

"It's not the Millers' place anymore, Edith. It's mine, and if I don't get some work done on it, I won't be out of your hair by Christmas." It was as good a reason as any to leave at nine o'clock at night during a wintry storm. The breaking news story about Nicolas Samuels was an even better one. No. Not Nicholas Samuels. *Eli Dougherty.* A child missing for nearly five years and now reunited with his father. Eli and the woman who'd called herself his mother had shown up in town a month before school began. They'd made no friends, had taken no interest in the community. Until Eli walked into the classroom where Maggie worked as a teacher's aide, he had been a complete stranger. It hadn't taken long for that to change. There'd been something about the solemn little boy that had tugged at Maggie's heart, and she'd spent extra time helping him with assignments and encouraging him to take part in playground activities. She'd also listened, really listened, to what he'd had to say about his life before he'd moved to Deer Park.

And now Eli's story was running on every local and national news station in the country.

Was that what Edith had been watching?

Maggie didn't dare ask.

No one could know about her part in the unfolding drama. Not Edith. Not Maggie's friends and coworkers. And most definitely not any of the reporters who were scouring Deer Park, Washington, searching for anyone willing to talk about the little boy and the woman who had been posing as his mother for five years.

"You've never been in my hair, and you know it. You're one of the best renters I've ever had, and I'll be happy to extend the rental contract for a few more weeks. Even months if you need the extra time," Edith said, and Maggie blinked, trying to refocus her attention on the conversation.

"You're sweet, but you and I both know that you have another renter lined up to move in the day after I leave." They'd discussed it several times in the month since Maggie had purchased the property outside of town.

"The renter is my grandson, and he can wait a few extra weeks. So, why don't you stay home for the night? We'll have popcorn and watch television together. Every single station is running the story about that little boy who was taken from his father five years ago. Can you believe he's been here for months and no one knew?"

"No. I can't."

"You've got to wonder how the police finally figured it out. One of the news stations said an anonymous source contacted them with information. Anonymous? Who stays anonymous unless they have something to hide? That's what I'm wondering? Maybe—"

"I've really got to go, Edith," Maggie cut in, her heart racing, her stomach churning. If Edith was asking those questions, plenty of other people would be, too. Journalists, newspaper reporters, television news anchors. People who would dig for answers until they found them. Until they found Maggie.

"I suppose you're right. If you're set on going, you shouldn't wait any longer. The storm is supposed to keep up all night, and the roads are only going to get more slippery. Be careful out there, you hear?"

"I will be."

"When will you be back?"

"Sunday night."

Maybe.

Or maybe she'd be halfway to somewhere else by then. Some other town, some other identity. Living a new life. Starting over.

Again.

Hot tears filled her eyes, but she refused to let them fall. She'd been through plenty in the past few years, and she'd survived. She'd survive this, too.

She hoped.

She jogged to her car, ice bouncing off her head and coat as she threw her duffel and satchel into the trunk. Edith was right. It *wasn't* a good night to be out. Maggie wanted to be tucked away in her attic apartment, grading tests. She wanted to take Edith up on the offer of popcorn and TV. More than anything she wanted to go back in time, make better choices, be the person she was now, *then*.

"But, you can't, so get over it. You made your mistakes and you're going to have to live with the consequences. Or die with them," she muttered as she pulled out onto the road.

Ice pinged off the car windows and bounced off the road, settling onto grass and trees and covering the asphalt with a layer of slippery moisture. The car fishtailed on the slick surface, and Maggie gripped the steering wheel with sweaty palms. She'd grown up in Florida, and even after three years of living in the Northwest, she still wasn't used to driving in icy weather.

So, why are you? Why not stay home instead of heading out into the storm? God has taken care of you for this long. Do you really think He's going to turn His back on you now?

She didn't.

Of course, she didn't.

But there was nothing wrong with being cautious. That's what going out to her country property was. Caution. Not lack of faith. Not fear.

"Right. Keep on telling yourself that, Maggie. Maybe by the end of the weekend, you'll believe it," she mumbled, her heart pounding frantically as the car fishtailed again. It had been a long day. A long few days. No way did she want to add a car accident to the stress. She needed to slow down, take a deep breath and concentrate on what she was doing.

She eased her foot off the gas, barely coasting as she turned onto the country lane that led to her new home. Tall pines and broad oaks shimmered in the darkness, dancing in the gusting wind and waving Maggie on. Years ago, someone had planted those oak trees. Someone had tended the fallow fields that lay beyond them. Now the five-mile stretch that led to Maggie's property was dark and lonely.

Maggie didn't care. The old farmhouse was everything she'd ever wanted. Large and airy with big rooms and turn-of-the-century charm, the place had been abandoned years ago. Would probably still be abandoned if Maggie hadn't gone on a country drive and seen it. Run-down, used up, lonely. Those were the things she'd thought when she'd looked at it, and she'd wanted to fix it up. Give it new life.

She'd thought she'd have plenty of time to do that.

And she would have if Eli hadn't walked into her life.

But he had, and everything had changed.

The car slid to the left, the tires spinning uselessly on ice and slush. Maggie tried to steer into the turn, but this time the car couldn't be righted. It slid across the road and nose-dived into a shallow ditch.

"Perfect." Maggie shoved open the door and scrambled out into the storm, shivering as cold wind speared through her coat and settled into her bones.

The front end of the car was tilted down, the wheels sunk deep into icy muck. If there was damage, Maggie couldn't see it, but she couldn't see a way to get the car out, either.

She pulled out her cell phone, dialed the local garage that had kept her aging Ford running for the past three years. It took several tries before someone answered, and Maggie frowned when she was told that it could take hours for the tow truck to arrive.

She could sit in the car and wait until then, or she could walk the rest of the way to the house. She stepped out into the street and stared down the road, trying to figure out how far she was from the farmhouse. There were no visible landmarks, just more pine and oak trees, more ice and silvery rain, but she was sure she'd traveled a few miles before she slid into the ditch. At most, she had another two miles to go. An easy walk on any other night, but a slippery one during a late-fall storm.

Still, she'd rather slip and slide all the way to the house than sit in the car imagining shadowy figures sneaking up from behind.

Imagining *him* sneaking up from behind.

She shuddered, grabbing her duffel and satchel from the trunk. The wind gusted, shaking needles and branches, the sound shivering along Maggie's nerves as she picked her way along the dark road. She'd never been afraid of the dark, never much worried about things that went bump in the night, but the storm gave life to the darkness, whipping shadows, bending pine boughs, whispering and whistling through the trees.

And no matter how much she told herself otherwise, no matter how much she reminded herself that she wasn't alone on the dark country road, that God was with her, guiding her, protecting her, Maggie *was* afraid.

Bright light speared through the darkness as the sound of a car engine mixed with the howl of wind and pinging ice. Maggie jumped to the side of the road, her feet slipping out from under her as she scrambled to move out of the way of the approaching vehicle. She went down hard, her breath leaving on a painful whoosh.

A car door slammed, footsteps crunched on ice, and Maggie twisted and managed to push to her feet, to face the person backlit by headlights.

Tall. Large muscular build. A man. She was sure of that. A hat covered hair that might have been any color, but Maggie imagined it was midnight black.

Black hair.

Black eyes.

Sinfully full lips that could smile or snarl depending on his mood.

Derrick?

For a moment, Maggie let panic take her, let it spear through her stomach and her mind until the only thought she had was escape. She took a step back, her feet slipping in ice and mud.

"Careful. You don't want to end up on the ground again."

The deep voice didn't belong to Derrick, and the hand that wrapped around her wrist, holding her steady as she regained her balance, was firm without being tight, controlled rather than cruel.

"You're right. Thanks." Her voice shook, and she cleared her throat, trying to quiet her frantic, panicked breathing.

"You're Maggie Tennyson, right?"

A journalist. He had to be. Somehow he'd found out about Maggie's part in reuniting Eli with his father, and he'd tracked her down. It wasn't good, but it was better than the alternative—Derrick standing in front of her, ready to mete out the vengeance he'd promised more than three years ago. "That's right."

"I thought so. Your landlady said you were heading to your country home. She seemed really concerned that you wouldn't make it. Something about threadbare tires and a lightweight car."

"I guess she was right to be worried, because the car ended up in a ditch," Maggie said, surprised that Edith would give out information to a stranger. But then, Edith did like being in the loop, and she'd love being part of one of Deer Park's biggest-ever news stories.

"Fortunately, mine is made for this kind of weather. How about I give you a ride to your place?"

"My mother always told me not to accept rides from strangers, and since I'm not far from home, I think I'll listen to her advice. Thanks, though. I appreciate the offer." She kept her voice light as she started to turn away.

"Maybe it'll help if I introduce myself. I'm Kane Dougherty. Eli's father."

Eli's father—the man who'd been searching for his missing child for five years and whose impassioned plea for his son's return had been replaying in the news since word of the father and son's reunion had broken that morning—was standing on the country road that led to Maggie's house.

And Maggie wished desperately that he wasn't.

"I asked the sheriff not to tell you who I was."

"And I told him that I needed to know. You brought me the miracle I've been praying for, and I wanted to thank you in person."

"I've never needed thanks for doing the right thing, Mr. Dougherty."

"Kane. And you may not need thanks, but I need to give it. How about I start by making sure you get to your place in one piece?"

There was no sense in refusing the ride, no way to undo the fact that Kane Dougherty was standing in front of her, so she nodded, trying to smile past the nerves that knotted her stomach. "Thanks. It's not far."

"It wouldn't matter if it was a thousand miles. I'd still be happy to do it." The words were suave and easy, the kind of thing a player might say to impress a lady, but there was sincerity in Kane's tone that Maggie couldn't deny.

He opened the car door, and the interior light went on, highlighting the black leather seats and the young boy who sat in the back. As always, Eli was still and watchful, his pale freckled face anxious and wary.

"Hello, Nicolas. Or do you want me to call you Eli now?"

"Eli, I guess." But he didn't look happy about it, and Maggie wondered how the transition was going for father and son.

"I missed you in school today," she said, sliding into the car and turning to face the nine-year-old boy.

"They said I couldn't go."

"Who said that?"

"My…" Eli shot a look in Kane's direction. "Father and

aunt and the police. They said there were too many people who wanted to talk to me and take my picture."

"They were right. You wouldn't want a bunch of strangers following you all over the school."

"I guess not, but now I'm going to have a lot of make-up work to do."

"Not so much. It is the day before Thanksgiving, after all. Mrs. Trenton didn't even assign homework."

"She didn't?"

"No. So you can stop worrying and enjoy your vacation." Maggie leaned over the seat and ruffled Eli's hair, then settled back into place as Kane rounded the car and got behind the steering wheel. She caught a flash of a strong jaw and high cheekbones, tan skin and deep-set eyes before the door closed and the interior light went off.

"I don't think Eli considers this a vacation. It's more a slow torture." Kane's voice was light, but Maggie heard the tension in it.

"Is it that bad, Eli?" She glanced over her shoulder, but Eli was staring out the window and didn't respond.

"He's had a rough couple of days. Haven't you, sport?" Kane started the engine and drove down the road, the silence that followed his comment thick and telling.

"It will get better," Maggie said, praying she was right. Eli had been taken from his home the previous morning and reunited with Kane less than twenty-four hours later. It was going to take time for him to adjust to his new circumstances. Time for him to realize that he really was where he belonged.

"You're right. And in the meantime, we thought it would be nice to come for a visit with one of his favorite teachers. Right, Eli?"

"She's my *only* favorite teacher."

"That's very sweet, Eli, and I'm happy for the visit, but it really isn't a good night to be out and about."

"I figured the weather would make it easier for me to get to you without bringing the press along. The sheriff said you'd like your role in things kept quiet and that you didn't want any part of the press."

"He's right." She'd asked Sheriff O'Malley not to mention her name to anyone. Including Kane. Apparently, he hadn't respected her wishes.

"It took me a while to get the information out of him, but I think, being a father himself, he couldn't deny me the chance to thank the person who gave me back my son." His voice had gone gritty with emotion, and Maggie touched his shoulder, felt the corded muscle beneath his coat and let her hand fall away.

The last thing she wanted to do was make a connection, allow herself to be pulled into the drama of Kane and Eli's life, pulled into the spotlight with them.

"Like I said before, I don't need thanks. I did what anyone would have."

"Then why didn't anyone? Why didn't…" He glanced in the rearview mirror and frowned. "I guess now isn't the time to discuss this."

"No, I guess not." Not with Eli sitting behind them, listening to every word.

"So, how about we discuss it over dinner Friday night?"

"I appreciate the offer, but I've got a busy weekend ahead of me. My driveway is to the right. At the white mailbox."

"I'd say that everyone has to eat, but that would be cliché. So how about I just suggest we do it another time?"

"I really can't, Kane."

"Because you want to stay away from the press?"

"Yes."

He was silent for a moment, and Maggie expected him to ask why that was so important to her.

Finally, he nodded. "Okay. So, how about we just meet out here again next weekend? I'll bring dinner, and we can chat."

"Next weekend?" He was staying in town that long? She'd thought that Kane and Eli would fly to Kane's New York home soon after their reunion and take their entourage of reporters with them.

And Maggie would be safe again.

"Unless you'd rather do it on a weeknight. We'll be moving into our rental on Monday—"

"Rental?"

"A few blocks north of the school. I asked Eli if he wanted to go back to New York now or wait until the end of the school year. He wants to wait. Right, bud?"

"Right." Eli's response was subdued, and Maggie wondered if he wanted to leave Deer Park, Washington, at all. He'd once told her that he'd lived in seven different states and attended the same number of schools. Shy and serious, he didn't make friends easily, and Maggie was sure the frequent moves had only made things more difficult.

"I'm glad you're staying until the end of the school year."

Even if that meant Maggie would have to leave.

"Me, too. I like it here. So, since I'm staying, *will* you have dinner with me and my father next weekend?"

"I…" *Can't* was on the tip of her tongue, but she couldn't say it without offering an excuse, and she didn't have one. "I'd love to. As long as nothing comes up between now and then."

Kane stopped in front of the old farmhouse, and Maggie

opened the car door, shivering as cold wind slapped her cheeks. "I guess we're here. Thanks for the ride."

"I'll walk you up." Kane got out of the car and walked around to escort her.

"I'm fine, Kane. I think it's best if you and Eli head back."

"We will, but before I go, I wanted to let you know that there's a hundred-thousand-dollar reward for information leading to Eli's recovery. It's yours."

"What?"

"The money is yours. My lawyer will transfer the funds to your account—"

"No."

"No?"

"I don't want money. That's not why I listened to Eli's story about having a father in New York, and it's not why I contacted the sheriff when I realized what he was saying might be true." She fished the keys from her purse, opened the front door, stepped inside and flipped on the foyer light.

"That doesn't mean the money isn't yours," he said, the light spilling over him, highlighting a face that belonged on a magazine cover. High cheek bones, a square jaw shadowed with stubble, lips that were full and firm. The wide brim of his hat threw shadows over eyes that were the same deep green as Eli's. Was his hair red like his son's?

"Look, I apprec—" Maggie's words were cut off as lights flashed at the end of her driveway. Someone was coming, and she didn't plan to stand in the doorway, waiting to find out who it was. "I need to go. Tell Eli I'll see him at school."

"Wait—"

But Maggie couldn't afford to wait. Not when the headlights were moving closer and anyone with a good camera could get a picture of her standing in the threshold chatting with Kane.

She slammed the door and turned the lock, stepping deeper into the house, wishing she could believe that would be enough to keep her hidden from the world, to preserve the life she'd fought so hard for.

Please, God, don't let it be a reporter, because I really don't want to leave Deer Park. I really don't want to have to start all over again.

She didn't want to, but she would.

Because if a photo of her somehow ended up in the news, if Derrick saw it, he'd come after her. There was no doubt about that.

And there was absolutely no doubt about what he'd do if he found her.

TWO

Maggie Tennyson had slammed the door in his face. After everything that had happened in the past twenty-four hours, Kane wasn't sure why that bothered him, but it did. He was tempted to knock, see if she would open the door again. He had a few questions he'd like to ask her.

Like—why was she so afraid of being in the spotlight? Why was she unwilling to accept the reward? Why did seeing a car pull into her driveway make her bolt?

He was tempted, but he wouldn't.

He had other things to worry about. Like reconnecting with his son.

Headlights splashed on the dirt driveway as Kane hurried back to the SUV he'd rented, and he eyed the approaching vehicle, wondering if it was possible that he had been followed from the hotel.

He might not understand Maggie's desire to stay anonymous, but he wanted to respect it. If a reporter did approach, Kane had no intention of mentioning Maggie's name or of explaining why he was at the property.

Of course, a good reporter would be able to find out who owned the farmhouse and might begin conjecturing about why Kane would bring Eli there.

To his relief, a tow truck pulled up beside the SUV and a gray-haired man got out. "Howdy. Maggie around?"

"She's inside."

"Glad to hear it. I nearly had a coronary when I got to her car and she wasn't in it. Weather's not good for taking a hike."

"I gave her a lift."

"Looks like her Ford isn't damaged, so you can tell Maggie that she's fine to drive it. Needs to put chains on the tires, though. Better yet, she should get new tires. Hers are looking threadbare, and that's not good for driving in the winter around these parts," he said almost absently as he unhooked the Ford.

"I'll let her know."

"Appreciate it. Tell her I'll bill her, or she can just drop into the shop and pay when she's got time." He finished the job and turned to face Kane again, his eyes narrowing as he caught sight of Eli peering out the window of the SUV. There was no doubt the driver recognized him. There probably wasn't a person in Deer Park who wouldn't have. Eli's image had been plastered across the front page of the local newspaper and featured on local and national news.

Kane braced himself for the comments and questions, the well wishes and speculations that he'd been hearing since he had arrived in town late the previous night.

Instead, the driver smiled at Eli, offered Kane a brief nod, got into his truck and drove away.

Would he spread the word that Kane and Eli had been visiting Maggie?

For her sake, Kane hoped not.

"Let's go give her the message, Dad." Eli climbed out of the car, brushing against Kane as he started walking toward the old farmhouse Maggie had disappeared into.

Kane wanted to put a hand on his son's shoulder, connect

with him in that small way, but he knew what Eli would do. He'd stiffen, holding himself tense and tight until Kane backed off. He wouldn't verbally protest the contact, but he wouldn't relax into it, either.

Give it time.

That's what the counselor who'd accompanied Kane to his first meeting with Eli had said. But Kane had already lost five years of his son's life. In that time, the bubbly four-year-old had turned into an anxious, unhappy little boy. It was a reality Kane had expected. One he'd thought he'd prepared for.

But how did a father prepare to meet a child he hadn't seen in five years? How did he reconcile memories with reality and balance his own need to connect with Eli's need to hold back and wait things out?

Kane didn't know, so he was simply going with the flow, taking it a minute at a time and praying he'd figure things out along the way.

He followed Eli up rickety porch steps and waited as he rang a doorbell that didn't seem to work.

Maggie must have been watching from one of the narrow windows that bracketed the door. Old wood creaked as it swung open, and she hovered at the threshold, smiling at Eli. "I thought you two were heading back to town."

Despite the smile, there was a nervousness about her, a tension in her muscles and her mouth that Kane didn't miss.

"We have a message for you, Ms. Tennyson. We came to deliver it," Eli replied in the overly formal way of his that Kane found both amusing and unsettling. Nine-year-old boys were supposed to be full of mischief and jokes. They were not supposed to speak like aged gentlemen.

"Well, then I guess you'd better come in and tell me

what it is." Maggie motioned for them to enter the house and quickly closed the door.

She'd taken off her coat, and the faded jeans and over-size flannel shirt she wore were as easy and comfortable as her smile. Golden-blond hair fell around her face in tangled waves that she brushed behind her ear, and Kane caught a whiff of a subtle, flowery perfume as she leaned a shoulder against the wall. She had an effortless beauty. The kind that didn't need makeup and fancy clothes to enhance it.

The kind that Kane had always found alluring.

"So, let's have it. What's the message?" she asked.

"Your car is back, and it's not damaged. You can drive it. And you'll get a bill for it, or you can go and pay for it next week."

"I always knew you had a good memory, Eli. Now, if you can just use it to memorize your multiplication facts while you're waiting to go back to school, you'll be all set." Her tone was gentle, her eyes a soft blue, her lips deep rose. All her attention was focused on Eli, and Kane suddenly understood why his son had been so desperate to visit Maggie. The combination of beauty and attentiveness would be a hard one for a kid like Eli to resist. It would be a hard one for anyone to resist.

"Maybe you could help me get them memorized," Eli said hopefully, and Maggie smiled again.

"I'm sure your father and aunt will want to do that."

"They're going to be busy getting the new house ready. They won't have time to help me."

"We'll always have time for you, Eli." Kane broke in, hoping he didn't look as disheartened as he felt. The transition into being a family again was going to be a rough one. He'd known that going into it. He'd hoped, though.

Hoped that Eli would be more eager to rebuild what they'd once had.

"I guess so." But Eli didn't look like he believed it.

"Guess so? Of course they will. You're the only reason they're in Deer Park, and I'm sure they'd much rather help you with math than get some stuffy old house ready."

Maggie's response was light and easy, but Kane didn't miss the concern in her eyes.

"Maybe. But you could help me, too. If I had three people helping, I'd be the best at multiplication in the whole school."

"You're quite a negotiator, aren't you? Maybe you'll grow up to be a lawyer."

A lawyer?

That's what Kane had been before he'd opened his P.I. firm, and it's what had nearly cost him his son. Prosecuting Lee Peyton and getting him convicted of murder had been the catalyst that sent Peyton's mother, Susannah, over the edge. Deprived of her only son, she'd decided to take Kane's. At least that's what the FBI agents working the case were speculating. Susannah Peyton wasn't talking. Whether she ever would was something Kane wouldn't speculate on.

"I want to be a detective. Like my father."

The comment surprised Kane, and he had to resist the urge to put a hand on Eli's shoulder, tell him how proud that made him feel. There was no sense in ruining the moment, and he knew from experience that physical contact with Eli would do just that.

"Sounds like an interesting career choice." Maggie glanced at Kane again, her expression guarded. Was she bothered by the fact that he was a private investigator? Or was she simply wishing he'd take Eli and leave?

"It has been," he offered, not nearly as anxious to go

back to the hotel as Maggie might be to have him leave. Eli's silence during the past few hours had weighed Kane down. Sports, school, friends, every subject he'd tried to discuss had been met with a one syllable response or no response at all. Maggie didn't seem to be having the same problem.

"I used to dream about being a private detective," she said, and Eli's eyes grew wide.

"Really?"

"Sure. I read just about every Nancy Drew and Hardy Boys book there was, and I wanted to be a teen detective just like them."

"Were you one?"

"No. I guess I forgot the dream for a while." Her smile faltered, and Kane wondered what memories had chased it away.

"So you're a teacher instead."

"Training to be one. Speaking of which, I have got some sugar cookies in the kitchen that I need a taste tester for."

"Taste tester?" Eli seemed intrigued, and Maggie offered him a hand, leading him down the hall.

"Sure. If you like them, then the other kids probably will, and I'll bring some in for a special treat one day."

"When I'm back at school?"

"Of course." Maggie pushed open a door, leading Eli into the room beyond.

Kane followed, feeling like a third wheel. He tried not to let it bother him. Maggie was a familiar face, a caring adult who'd listened to Eli when no one else would. Kane was a distant memory, a faded dream that Eli probably hadn't been sure was real. A dead man suddenly alive.

Kane would be scared, too, if he were in Eli's place.

He tried to keep that in mind as he walked into the

large kitchen. It was in a state of chaos. New cabinets, new floor, new paint. No countertop. No appliances. A large watermark stained the ceiling, and colorful glass tiles lay on a nicked table. A warped, cracked door let in gusts of cold air, and Kane had a feeling there were other cracks in other doors in the house. In windows. Maybe even in the roof.

Maggie might not want a monetary reward, but it was obvious she could use one.

"Excuse the mess. I'm still in the middle of renovations," she said as she reached into an upper cupboard, pulled out a package of cookies and offered one to Eli.

"It looks like you've done a lot already." Kane lifted one of the glass tiles, running his finger over the cool, smooth surface. "These are going to look good when they are up."

"I hope so. It took me forever to pick them out."

"You're planning to put them up this weekend?"

"Maybe, but first I've got a couple of windows and doors to put in."

"By yourself?"

"It's Thanksgiving weekend. My friends are celebrating with family, so that leaves me. If I want to be moved in by Christmas, I've got to work whether I have help or not."

"Why don't I see if I can hire a contractor to come in and finish the job for you?"

"No." Her tone was sharp, and she glanced at Eli, who'd already grabbed another cookie from the package. "I appreciate the offer, but I planned to spend the weekend working at my own pace and doing my own thing."

Kane wanted to argue. He wanted to remind Maggie that he owed her everything and that he'd be more than happy to make sure the entire house was renovated before her Christmas deadline.

Wanted to, but didn't.

She'd already made her position clear, so he kept quiet as she offered his son one more cookie.

His son.

Here in the room with him.

He'd prayed for this, hoped for it, but there had been a part of him that had given up believing that God would provide the miracle he'd wanted so desperately.

"Want one?" Maggie asked, holding out the cookies, her hand shaking a little.

Was she angry? Nervous? Scared?

Something was bothering her, that much was certain. He wanted to ask what, but Eli hovered a few feet away, slowly chewing his cookie and watching the exchange intently.

"No, thanks." Kane smiled, hoping to put Maggie at ease.

"I appreciate your bringing me the message about my car. When the tow truck pulled into the driveway, I was sure it was a reporter who'd followed you from the town."

"And that would have been bad news?"

"That's one way to put it." She offered a brief smile. "I don't suppose you got the name of the tow truck driver?"

"I'm afraid not. Is it important?"

"Probably not."

"But?"

"But I'd rather not have the news of your visit spread all over town. If Adam was the driver, he won't say anything to anyone. If he wasn't…" She shrugged.

"I didn't come here to cause you trouble, Maggie."

"You haven't. I just don't want any part of the media hype that's surrounding you. I've got a lot to do in the next few weeks, and the last thing I need are reporters camping around my property trying to get a story." Her voice was light, and Kane almost believed that was all there was to the story.

Almost believed it, but didn't.

He dealt with secrets every day. Big ones. Small ones. He knew when a person was hiding something, and Maggie was.

Right now, he had no choice but to let her keep her secrets, yet Kane had no intention of letting Maggie suffer because of the part she'd played in bringing Eli home.

"Okay."

"What do you mean, 'okay'?" she asked, frown lines marring her forehead.

"Just that you have a right to your privacy. Whatever your secrets are, I'm not going to try to uncover them. But if you're in trouble because of what you've done for my family, I'll do whatever it takes to help."

"Are you in trouble, Ms. Tennyson?" Eli asked, the cookie he was holding crumbling in his hand, and Kane could have kicked himself for giving his son more to be anxious about.

"Of course I'm not. Am I, Kane?" She frowned, spearing Kane with a disapproving stare.

"That was just a figure of speech, Eli. Ms. Tennyson isn't the kind of person to get into trouble."

Somehow, though, Kane had a feeling she *was* in trouble.

He wanted to push her for answers, find out what was really going on, but couldn't. Not with Eli listening. Kane would bide his time, wait until he had a chance to speak to Maggie alone, and then he'd try to get to the bottom of things. In the meantime, the best thing he could do was clear out of the house before word of his visit spread and she was inundated with the press she was so eager to avoid.

"You finished with those cookies, sport? Because I think it's time to head home."

"Can I have one more?"

Kane wanted to say yes. He wanted to give Eli everything in some vain attempt to make up for all the years he'd been unable to give him anything. That wasn't the way to build their relationship, though. God willing, he had a lifetime to live with his son, and the rules for their relationship needed to be set now rather than later. That meant being a father rather than a benevolent friend.

"You already had three. I think that's plenty."

"But they're my favorite."

"Then we'll pick some up at the store tomorrow."

"Tomorrow is Thanksgiving, and your parents are coming. We can't get cookies when they're here, can we?"

Your parents. Not *Granddad and Grandma.*

There was no connection between Eli and his grandparents, no shared holidays or birthdays that the boy could remember, nothing to make them more than strangers. But it still hurt to hear Eli refer to his grandparents in such an unemotional way.

"Sure we can. We'll just go in the morning before they arrive. Even if we can't, I'm sure Grandma won't mind doing a store run with us."

"Okay." Eli gave in easily enough, but that was the way he'd dealt with everything during the past twenty-four hours. Whether it was his nature, a learned behavior, or simply a response to a stressful and upsetting situation Kane didn't know. Would probably never know.

"Ready?" Kane held out his hand, his heart aching as Eli skirted by it and walked out of the kitchen.

"It must be incredibly wonderful to have your son back—and incredibly difficult to know he's not quite yours yet," Maggie said, neatly describing exactly what Kane felt. Elation. Sorrow. Joy. Pain. All of it mixed together in a confusing mass of emotions that Kane could only sometimes control.

"It is, but we'll make it through this. We'll get back to some kind of normal, and eventually we'll feel like a family again."

"I know you will. Eli is a wonderful little boy. He's going to be just fine." She walked out of the kitchen, and Kane followed, wishing he was as confident as Maggie seemed to be.

Time and patience. They were the key.

Kane just needed to keep that in mind as he navigated the new life he and Eli were forging together.

"You two be careful out there," Maggie said as she opened the door, stepping behind it so that she wouldn't be visible to anyone outside.

Was she hiding from someone?

If so, Kane wanted to know who.

He was tempted to go back to the hotel, log onto the Internet and do a search on Maggie Tennyson. Try to figure out what her secrets were and just how worried he should be for her.

Doing that would be a lot easier than trying to figure out the path that had taken Eli from chubby, happy toddler to quiet, solemn child. Figuring out where Eli had been, who he'd known, how it was possible that a kid whose picture had been on milk cartons and billboards, whose story had been in newspapers and on television, had escaped detection for so long, was something that Kane had to do. For his sake. For Eli's.

Kane had learned a lot in the past decade. He'd learned that grief wasn't fatal. He'd learned that life continued no matter how much a person might not want it to. Losing his wife had taught him that. Losing Eli had reinforced it. Now he'd been given a second chance, and he wouldn't waste it burying his head in the sand and ignoring what his son had been through.

He opened the car door for Eli, waited as he climbed in and then shut it again. As he rounded the SUV, his gaze was drawn to Maggie's farmhouse. She'd closed the front door, but light spilled out from a downstairs window. As Kane watched, a figure passed in front of it. Quickly. Furtively.

Maggie.

The woman who'd listened to Eli, who'd cared enough to go to the police when no one else had, had secrets that she didn't want to share. He was sure of that.

Maybe he should leave her to them, but Maggie had stepped in when others had stepped back. She'd listened to Eli's story about having another name and another home, and she'd acted on what she'd heard. She'd been the catalyst that had brought Kane's family back together. That was something Kane would never forget and could never repay. If what she'd done had caused her trouble, he'd do whatever it took to help her.

If she let him.

And based on the way she'd acted when they'd met, Kane doubted she would.

He got in the car and backed out of the driveway, Eli's silence filling the darkness. Was this what they were destined for? Long silences and stilted conversation.

Kane refused to believe it. God hadn't brought them this far to leave them floundering. There would be healing. There would be a future filled with all the things they'd missed out on during the past five years. As Kane drove toward the hotel, he tried to take comfort in that.

THREE

Maggie paced the bedroom at the top of the stairs, her stomach churning with dread. She needed to lie down on the inflatable mattress, close her eyes and try to sleep, but sleep didn't come easily on the best of nights.

And this definitely wasn't the best of nights.

As a matter of fact, Maggie figured it rated right up there with one of the worst.

No good deed ever goes unpunished.

She could almost hear her grandmother's raspy, smoker's voice, could almost see her wrinkled face and time-ravaged body sitting in the dark corner of the room, watching through still-sharp eyes.

"That's a wonderful image to have in the middle of a storm, in the middle of one of the worst nights of your life," she muttered, shivering a little as a gust of wind rattled the window and shot through its old frame. It was one of the windows she planned to replace. Maybe she shouldn't bother.

Maybe she should have a Realtor come and re-hang the "for sale" sign that had caught Maggie's eye nearly four months ago. Then Maggie could get in her car and drive back through the mountains, back down into the open land that she'd passed through when she'd run from Miami three years ago.

When she'd run from Derrick, the man she'd once believed herself madly in love with.

She was older now, hopefully wiser, and she knew the truth about love. It was fickle, blind and dumb. Pursuing it was a waste of time and energy, and when Maggie left Miami, she'd decided to put her efforts into something more concrete. Education, financial security, creating the kind of life she could be proud of.

And she had.

She was.

With God's help she'd pulled out of the downward spiral that had nearly killed her. She'd given up the party-hard lifestyle, and she'd finally found a measure of the peace she'd wanted so desperately when she was a young kid.

And now it was slipping through her fingers like mist on a summer morning.

One little boy with sad eyes and a wary demeanor, and Maggie had gotten herself embroiled in the biggest feel-good story of the year.

Feel-good for everyone but her.

If it weren't so awful, she'd laugh.

She sighed, rubbing the back of her neck, trying to ease the tension there. God had reasons for everything. Maggie believed that. Just as she believed that going to Sheriff O'Malley with her suspicions about Eli had been the right thing to do.

No good deed goes unpunished.

Maybe Grandma Jane had been right, but Maggie wouldn't change what she'd done. Seeing Eli with his father had been one of the best gifts she'd ever received. Sure, it had been difficult to observe the tension between the two, but Maggie had no doubt that Kane would eventually win his son over. The man had determination and patience to spare. She'd seen that in the way he'd stood back and let his son just be. No pressure. No expectations. He was going easy, not demanding anything from his confused little boy.

Maggie couldn't help but admire that.

Her cell phone rang, its shrill tone making her jump. She grabbed it, her heart beating rapidly as she glanced at the caller ID. It was after midnight, and Edith was calling. That couldn't be good.

She braced herself as she lifted the phone to her ear. "Hello?"

"Did I wake you, Maggie? I wasn't going to call, but it's just so exciting, I couldn't help myself."

"Exciting? What's exciting?"

"Well, first of all, the fact that Kane Dougherty showed up on my doorstep a few hours ago. You know who he is, right?"

Maggie considered playing dumb but knew Edith wouldn't fall for it. "He's the father of the little boy who was missing for five years."

"Exactly. And he was here looking for you. He said it was imperative that he speak to you. Did he make it out to the house?"

"Yes, he did." And Maggie had no intention of saying more than that.

"I'm not nosey enough to *ask* why he wanted to find you, but I'd be tempted to hint broadly that after three years of renting an apartment from me, you could trust me with any tidbit of information you wanted to throw my way."

Maggie laughed, some of her tension easing away. "Fine. I'll throw a tidbit your way. Kane's son is one of the students in my classroom."

"And?"

Maggie hesitated. She didn't want to lie, but she wasn't ready to tell Edith everything. "Eli was feeling unsettled, and Kane thought it would be good for him to see someone familiar."

"Makes sense. That poor child has been through a lot. Too much."

"Hopefully, things will be better for him now that he's back with his father."

"No doubt they will. I still can't believe that woman was right under our noses, and we didn't know it. A kidnapper in our midst."

"She hasn't been here long, and I don't think anyone got to know her. That made it easy for her to hide who she was and what she'd done."

"I suppose you're right. They showed a photo of her on the evening news, and I don't recall ever seeing her in town. Showed a photo of the little boy, too. Guess who was in the picture with him?"

Maggie's heart stuttered, then started up again. "Who?"

Please, don't say "you." Please don't.

"You!"

She said it, and Maggie's heart sank, her stomach tying in a knot so tight she could barely breathe let alone speak.

"Maggie? Did you hear me? You're famous!"

"I heard."

"Well, you don't sound very happy about it."

"I just don't understand where they got a photo of me, or why they'd put it on the news."

"It was taken at the harvest party at school. You were supervising some sort of game, and Eli was standing right next to you. I guess the parents of one of his classmates took the photo and sold it for a good price."

"I guess so."

"Don't sound so glum. This is great."

"It is?"

"I've had at least a dozen people call me to ask if it was really you in that picture. You're headline news here in Deer Park, and that means every eligible guy in the area will want to find out more about you."

Maggie laughed again, but this time the sound was hollow and empty. "Edith, you never give up, do you?"

"On finding Mr. Right for a good friend? I'm afraid not."

"For me, there is no Mr. Right."

"You're too young to be so cynical. Sometimes a girl has to kiss a lot of frogs before she finds her prince."

"And sometimes every frog she kisses is a toad," Maggie responded, only half listening to Edith.

She'd spent the better part of the day planning ways of staying out of the news, had driven out to the farmhouse in the first storm of the season to avoid cameras and reporters, and she'd been undone by a photo snapped at the class harvest party nearly a month ago.

"Okay, so maybe there *are* a lot of toads, but what if the next one is a prince? What if he's just waiting for his true love to appear? For all you know, he could sweep you off your feet tomorrow because he saw you in the news today."

"Edith, you read way too many romance novels."

"Romance novels? I'll have you know I lived the greatest romance of all. Can I help it if I want the same for the people I care about?"

"No. And I love you for it, but I'm not looking for Mr. Right, and I never will be."

"That doesn't mean you won't find him. God has His ways, you know."

Maggie did. She just didn't understand them. "Right. When was the photo in the news?"

"Eight o'clock is what Margaret said. She called me right afterward to tell me, but I wasn't sure I could believe her. Her eyes aren't as good as they used to be."

"When did you see it?"

"Ten o'clock. I was going to call you right away, but I got so many phone calls, I couldn't."

"Was it the local news?"

"Nope. You're famous countrywide. Probably farther. This story is a big one."

"That's for sure," she muttered, grabbing the few things she'd taken from her duffel and shoving them back inside it. Her first instinct had been right. She needed to leave town, get as far away from Deer Park and its sensational news as she could.

"Are you okay, dear? You sound…agitated."

For a moment, Maggie considered telling Edith that she was terrified, not agitated, but she didn't dare drag someone she cared about into her troubles. "I'm fine. I'm just surprised so many people noticed me in the photo."

"Noticed? You were a showstopper. Let me tell you. All that honey-blond hair hanging around your shoulders and the sweet smile you were giving that poor little boy. You looked breathtaking. There isn't a man on this planet who wouldn't want to get to know you, and there isn't a woman who isn't going to wish she was you."

"You're exaggerating, Edith."

"I'm not. Though I admit to a certain amount of bias when it comes to you. You're like one of my children, my dear, and I couldn't be prouder to know you."

Maggie's throat tightened at the words, her eyes filling with tears. If she could have chosen a mother, she would have chosen one like Edith. A woman who had devoted her life to her husband and children rather than to drugs and booze and the next creep with a wallet. "Thank you, Edith. That means a lot to me."

"Good. Now, let's stop being sappy and start planning what you're going to wear Sunday."

"Sunday?"

"To church, dear. You've got to look your best just in case—"

"Mr. Right has somehow magically appeared in town? How about we discuss this another time, Edith? It's late, and I'm tired." And she needed to leave, walk away from everything she'd worked so hard for.

"You're right. It *is* late, and we both need our beauty sleep. Call me tomorrow, okay?"

"Okay." But she wouldn't because she'd be hundreds of miles away, trying to find a new identity so that she could sink into obscurity again. She hung up the phone, her muscles leaden and tight as she grabbed her duffel and walked out of the room. She'd leave the satchel with the grade book and ungraded papers. Eventually, someone would come looking for her and find it.

The stairs creaked as she hurried down, the old floorboards groaning beneath her feet as she rushed into the kitchen and scrounged through the cupboards. She didn't have much. Just a package of crackers, a couple of cans of soup and the cookies she'd shared with Eli a few hours ago. She grabbed one and took a bite as she shoved everything else into her duffel. It tasted like dust, and she nearly choked as she tried to swallow it down.

Sugar could cure a lot of ills, but it did nothing to tame the fear that beat a hard, harsh rhythm in Maggie's chest. Her picture was on national news programs, and Derrick had always been a news fanatic. Wall Street news. Cable news. Network news. He'd watched it incessantly, and

Maggie had often been jealous that he hadn't spent that time with her.

She'd been such a fool, so confused about what real love was, what true caring felt like.

And now she was going to pay the price.

Again.

She frowned, hurrying back down the hall, silently saying goodbye to the house she'd scrimped and saved to purchase, the dream she'd built in her head.

She pulled open the front door, stepping out onto the porch, the cold wind bathing her hot cheeks and drying the tears that burned behind her eyes. Ice had accumulated on the front porch, and the yard and driveway sparkled with it. Tall pine trees bent beneath the howling wind, and ice fell from their heavy boughs, hitting the ground with a hushed shattering that was so beautiful, so achingly perfect that Maggie paused, wanting to take it all in, preserve the memory so that she would never forget what was possible if she put her mind and heart into it.

A sharp crack split the air as something exploded near Maggie's feet. Wood flew up and out, digging into her shins, flying into her face. She screamed, falling backward.

Another crack. Another explosion.

Pain.

Blood. Dripping down her arm. Dripping onto the rotted wooden floorboards of the porch.

She screamed again, scrambling back as a figure appeared in the darkness beyond the porch. A hundred yards away. Coming fast.

Get up! Get. Up.

The world in slow motion as she turned, fell into the hallway, kicked the door shut. Hands slipping as she turned the lock. Pulled the bolt. Blood smeared on the door.

Go. Go, go, go.

She ran up the stairs, expecting the door to explode behind her. Expecting a bullet to slam into her back, bring her to her knees.

Her cell phone slipped out of her hands as she pulled it from her pocket, and she scooped it up again. She tried desperately to dial 911, her hand trembling too much. Fingers hitting the wrong buttons.

Please, God. Please!

A loud bang had her screaming again, lunging for the bedroom door, slamming it shut, turning the old-fashioned skeleton key as the 9-1-1 operator answered.

Another bang as Maggie shouted her address, shouted that an intruder was in her house.

And then silence, deep and ominous and filled with warning.

"Ma'am? Are you still there? Can you hear me?"

"Yes," Maggie responded, backing away from the bedroom door, her heart thudding a hard, painful beat.

Was he in the house? Creeping up the stairs? Standing outside the door?

"Police are in route. Are you in a safe place?"

"No."

"Can you get to one?"

"No."

Was that the loose floorboard on the landing creaking? Was that a whisper of fabric, a sigh of breath?

"Do you have a weapon?"

"No," she barely managed to whisper, as she glanced around the room, trying to find something she could use to defend herself.

"The police are almost there. Stay on the phone with me, okay? Okay?"

But Maggie couldn't respond, didn't dare speak or move or breathe. Someone *was* outside the door. Someone who tapped softly on the thick wood, wiggled the handle as the sound of sirens drifted into the room.

Maggie backed up, moving toward the window, dizzy with fear, sick with it. Waiting for help to come, for the door to explode. For Derrick to appear. Black eyes and hair and snarling lips. Coming to do exactly what he promised he would when Maggie had walked out of his life.

But she wasn't the woman she'd been all those years ago. She'd changed. Grown stronger, more determined, and she wasn't going to wait around for whoever was on the other side of the door to break in and finish what he'd started.

She yanked open the window, eyeing the ground as sirens screamed up her driveway. Voices shouted. A gunshot split the air.

And then there was silence filled with nothing but wind and ice and the terrible beat of Maggie's heart.

FOUR

Kane hovered in the doorway of the hotel suite's only bedroom, watching as Eli climbed into bed. He wanted to cross the threshold and tuck his son in as he had so many times when Eli was little, but the dark look Eli shot in his direction froze him in place.

Give him time.

It was what Kane's mother and father had said. What his sister had said. What the experts had said. It wasn't what Kane's heart said. *It* said fix everything now. Swoop in and take control like he'd done when he'd worked as an attorney. But reconnecting with Eli was going to be a lot more difficult than bringing a case to trial had ever been.

At least he'd finally gotten the kid to bathe and get ready for bed. That had been a battle Kane hadn't expected to fight with a child Eli's age. Only seeing the panic in Eli's eyes when sleep had been mentioned had kept Kane from insisting that his son go to bed at a reasonable time.

Now, at nearly one in the morning, Eli's excitement and adrenaline seemed to have worn off, and his pale face and the dark circles beneath his eyes hinted at an exhaustion that went far beyond simple lack of sleep.

"Do you want a drink of water?" Kane asked, the question as lame and useless as he felt.

"No. Thank you." Eli turned onto his side so that his back was to Kane, his red hair just showing over the blanket he'd pulled up around his shoulders.

That was Kane's cue to walk away. He knew it but couldn't quite get his feet to move.

"What time does Mom and Dad's plane arrive tomorrow?" his sister Jenna asked, and Kane forced himself to turn away from his son and face her.

The look of sympathy on her face let him know just how pitiful he looked—a father who couldn't even offer his son a kiss goodnight. "Ten."

"Do they want me to pick them up at the airport?"

"No, they're renting a car." Kane moved across the room, grabbing the cup of coffee he'd left on a corner table. It was cold and bitter, but he downed it anyway, his throat parched from too many emotions and the strain of holding them in.

"Keep drinking coffee and you'll never get to sleep." Jenna rose from the couch, stretched to her full five-foot height. Short red hair spiked around a pale, pretty face. She looked exhausted.

"I'm too hyped up to sleep."

"Maybe so, but we've been up since yesterday morning. It's time to crash. Tomorrow is another day, after all, and I'm sure we'll have plenty that needs doing." She ran a hand over her hair and smiled. Of Kane's three sisters, Jenna was the only one still single and childless, and she'd been quick to volunteer to hop on a plane and fly to Spokane, Washington, with him. It had been Jenna who'd booked a hotel room. Jenna who'd thought to rent the SUV. Jenna who had been the calm in the storm of Kane's emotions, but two years fighting leukemia had taken a lot out of her, and it showed in her hollow cheeks and dark-rimmed eyes.

He crossed the room and pulled her into a gentle hug.

She'd always been athletic and strong, a gymnast who'd pushed her body to the limit and who'd attended college on a full athletic scholarship. Now she was frail, her body too thin and delicate. "I'm sorry."

"For what?" She returned the hug and stepped back, looking up into his eyes.

"For not thinking about how difficult this trip would be on you."

"On me? What about you? You're the one who's just found his son again." She frowned, and Kane knew she would never admit that the cancer had robbed her of her strength, never admit that was the reason she was tired. She was strong, tough and independent, and the last thing she would ever accept was pity.

"True, but I'm still hopped up on adrenaline, and there's no way I can sleep. You take the other double bed in the bedroom. I'll take the pull-out in here."

"I'm sure you want to be in the room with Eli," she responded, crossing to the small refrigerator and pulling out a bottle of water.

True, but he wasn't sure his son wanted him there.

He didn't say that, just poured more coffee from a half-full pot and shook his head. "I'll only be a few yards away from him, and you can get some sleep while I do some work. I've got a half-dozen clients I left hanging when I flew out of New York, and I need to let them know their cases are still being handled."

"All right, but if you want to boot me out of bed later, just wake me up." She smiled wanly, and for the first time since they'd gotten on the plane the previous day, Kane really looked at his sister. Her skin wasn't just pale, it was parchment white, her freckles standing out in stark contrast. Her clothes hung off her narrow frame.

"Are you okay, Jen?"

"Besides being exhausted? Yes."

"I mean *really* okay."

"You *mean* is the cancer back. I went to the doctor two weeks ago for a three-month check, and my numbers all look great, so stop worrying."

"Did the doctor say anything else besides that your numbers look good?"

"No, and even if he had, now wouldn't be the time to discuss it. You have your son back, Kane. You've got what you've been dreaming of for years. That's all you should be thinking about."

"I have what I've been dreaming of, but that doesn't mean I can't worry about you. So, what, exactly, did the doctor say?"

"Nothing except come back in three months. Just like every checkup. Now, stop worrying."

A sharp knock at the door stopped Kane from asking more questions. He frowned, crossing the room quickly and peering out the peephole. Up until now, the press had been respectful, waiting outside the hotel and asking questions when he emerged or calling to see if he'd be willing to give an interview, but he didn't expect that to last forever. "Yes?"

"Mr. Dougherty, it's Deputy Rick Lesnever, Spokane County Sheriff's department."

"Do you have ID?" Kane asked, opening the door and nodding as the deputy flashed his badge. "It's a little late for a visit isn't it, Deputy?"

"We've had an incident, and the sheriff wanted me to come ask you a few questions." The deputy was young, maybe mid-twenties, and he looked nervous, his gaze jumping from Kane to Jenna and back again.

"Incident?" Kane asked, stepping aside and letting the man in.

"Maggie Tennyson said you were out at her place a little after nine tonight."

"That's right."

"She was attacked a couple hours later."

"Attacked by whom?" Kane asked, his mind racing back to the moment he'd met Maggie. She'd been nervous, edgy and scared, but he'd chalked that up to being approached by a stranger on a dark, deserted road. What he hadn't been able to explain was her need to stay anonymous, her obvious concern that someone would know Kane and Eli had been to visit her.

He'd wondered what she was hiding, but he hadn't pushed for answers.

He should have.

"We don't know. We're hoping that you might be able to help shed some light on that."

"You don't think my brother had something to do with it?!" Jenna exclaimed, her eyes flashing with irritation.

"Mr. Dougherty isn't a suspect, but we're hoping that he may have seen something—"

"What's going on? Is Ms. Tennyson okay?" Eli peered out of the bedroom, his hair mussed. Barely four feet tall and probably less than fifty pounds, Eli looked younger than nine, but his eyes were old and filled with anxiety.

"She should be fine," the deputy responded, smiling kindly at Eli. "We just wanted to ask your father a few questions."

"But you said she was attacked. That means someone hurt her." Eli stepped out of the room, his pajamas hanging loosely on his thin frame.

"Maybe you and the deputy should discuss this some-where else," Jenna suggested, shooting a look in Eli's direction.

She was right, of course. Discussing what had happened

to Eli's favorite teacher while he was listening wasn't a good idea, but leaving Eli seemed like an even worse one to Kane.

He knew it was irrational, knew that Eli would be fine with Jenna for however long it took to answer Deputy Lesnever's questions, but knowing it in his head and believing it with his heart were two different things. "Why don't you go back in the bedroom, Eli? I'll come in after the deputy and I are done talking and let you know what's going on."

"She's not okay. If she was okay, you wouldn't make me go away while you talk."

"Of course she's okay. Deputy Lesnever wouldn't lie, would you, Deputy?" Jenna said, moving close to Eli and putting an arm around his shoulders.

"No, I wouldn't. She's fine. The doctors are keeping her in the hospital overnight for observation, but she'll probably be going home tomorrow."

"She's in the hospital? But you said she was all right!" Eli's voice rose an octave, and he shrugged away from Jenna's arm.

"She is, but—"

"I really think you should discuss this somewhere else," Jenna said again, and this time Kane knew he had to listen. Eli had been through enough. He didn't need to hear details about what had happened to Maggie.

"How about we step out in the hall?"

"I'd rather not stand in a public area. We can discuss things in my patrol car."

Kane hesitated, then nodded. He couldn't be near Eli 24/7 no matter how much he wanted to. Normalcy had to be established. Routine. If Kane hovered, he might do more damage to his already-damaged child.

"Will you go see Ms. Tennyson?" Eli asked.

"I don't think—"

"Please, Daddy. I just want to know for sure that she's all right."

Daddy?

The word brought Kane back five years to the morning of Eli's disappearance. He'd kissed his son goodbye before heading to the office, smiling when his son shouted, "I love you, Daddy!" as Kane closed the apartment door and left him with the nanny.

He hadn't heard the word again until now, and hearing it filled him with a bittersweet mixture of joy and sorrow.

"I can't leave you here alone, Eli."

"He won't be alone, Kane. I'm here, and I promise this is where we'll both stay. No going anywhere except to bed. Right, Eli?" Jenna offered, and Eli nodded his agreement. Kane hesitated, his thoughts going back to the old farmhouse and the woman who owned it. Maggie Tennyson had done what no one else had dared. She'd listened to Eli, dug for answer and found them. Now she was in the hospital, and Kane knew he couldn't ignore the fact any more than he could ignore his son's impassioned plea.

"Okay. I'll go, but you have to mind your aunt while I'm gone. No wandering around outside. Okay?"

Eli nodded, his desire to communicate with Kane gone now that he'd achieved his goal.

Had he spent the past five years as silently as he'd spent the past day? Or had he formed a connection with his kidnapper, spent afternoons after school chatting and weekends hanging out and discussing plans for the new week?

Wondering how Eli had spent the past five years would torture Kane if he let it. He couldn't let it. He stepped over and hugged Eli, his heart aching as Eli stiffened in his arms. "Goodnight, buddy. I love you."

Eli didn't respond, just turned and walked back into the bedroom.

Kane bit back a sigh, and met Jenna's eyes. "I won't be long."

"Take your time. We'll be fine while you're gone."

"Thanks. Get some sleep. Okay." He dropped a kiss on Jenna's cheek and followed the deputy out into the hall.

"Sorry to drag you away from your son like this, Mr. Dougherty."

"Call me Kane, and don't worry about it. I'm happy to help with the investigation any way I can, though I'm not sure there's much I can tell you."

"Whatever you remember from when you were out at the house will be just fine."

They walked out into the icy storm, crossed the parking lot to the deputy's cruiser and climbed in. If there were reporters hanging around, Kane didn't see any, but, then, even the most diehard reporters were probably tucked away in their hotel rooms sleeping at this hour of the morning.

Kane waited impatiently as the deputy pulled out a notebook and tried two different pens before finally finding one that worked. "Okay, I'm set. Did you see anything or anyone while you were at Maggie's place?"

"Just the tow truck driver."

"Tow truck driver?"

"He was dropping off Maggie's car. It had slid off the road and into a ditch."

"Did you get the name of the driver?"

"Maggie mentioned the name Adam, but I'm not sure that was him."

"Was he still there when you left?"

"No, and he never even spoke to Maggie. Just left the car and took off."

"And you saw no one else?"

"No. There wasn't a car on the road on my way back here. It's not a good night to be out."

"It isn't, but that didn't stop you and someone else from getting to Maggie's place."

"You said she was attacked. What happened?"

"She was shot."

"Shot?" It wasn't an attack then. It was an attempted murder. Imagining Maggie lying in her house wounded and scared, made him want to find the shooter and teach him a lesson he wouldn't soon forget.

"Yeah. She was lucky, though. The bullet went through the fleshy part of her shoulder, and the doc says she'll make a full recovery."

"Did she see the guy who did it?"

"I'm afraid not."

"Does she have any idea who it might be?"

"I'm not at liberty to say." Which meant Maggie had an idea, but the deputy didn't plan to share it.

That was fine. Kane was more than willing to ask Maggie the same question.

"Which hospital was she taken to?"

"Spokane Valley. It's a thirty-minute drive, though, so you may want to wait until tomorrow to visit her."

"I told Eli I'd check on her, and that's what I plan to do."

"Why don't I escort you over there then? I'm heading in that direction anyway."

"Thanks. I'm sorry I couldn't be of more help."

"If you think of anything else, give the sheriff's office a call."

"I will." Kane got out of the cruiser and hurried to his rental, his mind spinning with possibilities. Maggie had seemed nervous and scared when they'd met. That, combined with the deputy's refusal to answer Kane's question about whether or not she'd had any idea who'd shot her, indicated that there was something more going on than a random attack.

Had the attack happened because of what she'd done for Kane and Eli?

She'd made it very clear she didn't want her picture in the news, and it had been. Kane had seen her in a photo that had flashed across the television screen while Eli was getting ready for bed.

Had that been what led to the attack?

Kane didn't know, but he planned to find out. Maggie might not want his help, but he owed it to her, and he'd do whatever it took to make sure she stayed safe.

FIVE

Maggie hated hospitals. The scents, the sounds, the hushed anticipation that always seemed to hang in the air. People suffered in hospitals. They died there. She'd watched her grandmother breathe her last breath on a sterile hospital gurney. She'd sat beside her mother's hospital bed one too many times after she'd overdosed on drugs and been rushed to the emergency room. Four years ago, Maggie had followed an ambulance as it brought her mother's nearly lifeless body to the hospital for one last futile attempt to resuscitate. She'd promised herself then that she wouldn't follow in her mother's footsteps. She'd given up drugs, given up alcohol, given up the hard-partying lifestyle that had led her to Derrick.

That had been the beginning of the end of their relationship.

But it hadn't been over.

Maggie had known too much about Derrick's business. Not the car dealership that he claimed made him millions, but the illicit drug trade that he'd been part of. He hadn't planned on letting her walk away from their relationship. She'd known it as surely as she'd known that going to the police with information about Derrick's drug connections would be futile. She'd tried anyway, hoping that what she knew would put Derrick away for the rest of his life. He hadn't even been put away for a day, and he'd vowed to repay her for her betrayal. She'd known he meant it, and she'd run, hoping that putting distance between them would keep her safe.

And now she was pacing a sterile hospital room, trying desperately to believe that the person who'd shot her hadn't been sent by Derrick.

She shuddered, glancing at the closed door and wishing there was a lock she could turn to keep danger out.

But there isn't, so do the smart thing and leave. She turned quickly, swaying from a combination of blood loss and pain medication. She was fuzzy-headed, but not so fuzzy-headed that she didn't know what staying in the hospital room made her—a sitting duck.

Her duffel bag was lying on the chair where a kind nurse had left it, and Maggie scrounged through it, pulling out a pair of gray corduroy pants and a white three-button sweater that she thought she could wiggle into, shoulder bandages and all.

It didn't take long to change from the hospital gown into street clothes, and Maggie managed to scrape her hair into a ponytail and shove her feet into sneakers with barely a twinge from her gunshot wound. Maybe adrenaline deadened pain, or maybe the pain meds she'd been given really were doing their job. Either way, Maggie planned to find a way out of town before the effects wore off.

She grabbed the duffel, checked to make sure her wallet was inside and left the room, her stomach sick with the reality of what she was doing. Soon she'd be leaving everything behind. Her friends. Her church. Her job.

Eli.

How would he feel when he found she was gone?

The question followed her as she stepped into the

corridor and walked to the nurses' station. A twenty-something nurse smiled as Maggie approached. "Can I help you?"

"I'm Maggie Tennyson. Room 509. I've decided not to stay the night. Can you let my doctor know?"

"You can't leave." She looked appalled, her deep-brown eyes wide with concern.

"Yes. I can."

"Dr. Stevenson wanted to run another blood panel before you leave. If you wait in your room, I'll see if we can do that now rather than tomorrow morning."

"I can't wait. Thank you, though."

"But—"

"I appreciate the wonderful care I've had while I was here, but I really do think I'll be more comfortable at home." Maggie smiled and turned away, hurrying to the elevator across from the nurses' station, slamming her finger on the button, half afraid security personnel would swoop in and force her back to the room.

The door opened, and she stepped in, pushing the button for the lobby and feeling like a criminal escaping the scene of a crime. Would someone be waiting below to escort her back up?

Of course not. It was a free country, after all. She hadn't committed a crime, and there was no reason why she couldn't go where she wanted when she wanted.

She straightened her shoulders, stepped off the elevator and straight into a warm, hard chest. She stumbled back, nearly falling as she struggled to regain her balance.

"Careful." Hands cupped her upper arms, holding her in place, and she looked up into the calm, handsome face of Kane Dougherty.

"Kane! What are you doing here?"

"I could ask you the same question. Last I heard, you'd

been admitted and were staying the night." He studied her face, his eyes deep emerald, his dark hair wet from rain and melting ice.

Maggie's breath caught, the slow tumble of her stomach, the quick throb of her pulse, surprising her. She could not be attracted to Kane. She would not be. She'd learned her lesson about love a long time ago. She didn't plan to forget it.

"Who did you hear that from? I haven't even called Edith, yet."

"A deputy came to see me. He said you'd been shot."

"Barely."

"I didn't realize that was possible." He cocked his head to the side, the angle of his jaw, the shape of his eyes, the intent, solemn look on his face reminding her of Eli. But Kane was no boy. He was a full-grown, good-looking, trouble-causing man.

She didn't need to know him to know that.

There hadn't been a man in Maggie's life who hadn't caused more trouble than he was worth.

"Didn't realize what was possible?"

"To be barely shot. I figure a person either *is* shot or she isn't." He offered a quick smile.

"The doctor says I'll heal completely. And, really, it barely hurts."

"Maybe not, but you look pale. Are you sure you should be leaving the hospital?"

"I'll recuperate better at home in my own bed." Or in a hotel room where no one could find her. Not Kane. Not the police.

Not Derrick.

She started to cross the lobby, but Kane put a hand on her arm, his fingers warm and compelling through her cardigan. "You're running from something, Maggie. What is it?"

"I don't know what you're talking about."

"Of course you do. You were running when I found you walking along the road, and you're running now. Who's after you?"

"Why does someone have to be after me? Why can't I just be a woman who wants a little time alone?" she asked, refusing to let herself be pulled into offering excuses. She didn't owe Kane any.

"Because you were scared when we met, and you're scared now. And because someone shot you a couple of hours after your photo was in the news. That isn't coincidence, is it, Maggie? You were hiding from someone, and now he's found you."

Shocked, she didn't know what to say. She didn't know if she should admit the truth or keep trying to hide it.

Finally, she did the only thing she could.

"Look, Kane, you and Eli have enough to deal with. You don't need to add my troubles into the mix. Go back to the hotel, go back to your son and stop worrying about me."

"That's not possible. What you did for me and for Eli makes you family, and I never turn my back on family."

"You're wrong. I'm not family. I'm just a stranger who happened to touch your lives for a little while. In a few days, you'll forget I even exist." She tugged away from his hand, walked to the automatic doors and stepped out into the freezing rain, her chest hot and tight with emotions she didn't want to feel.

There had been so many times in her life when she'd longed to hear someone say what Kane had. So many times when all she'd wanted was to be part of a loving family.

"Do you have a ride?" He walked up behind her but

didn't touch her again, didn't ask why she was running, where she was going, didn't mention family.

"No. I guess I wasn't thinking very far ahead."

"Then I guess it's good I'm here. Where are you heading?"

The bus station, the airport, the train station. Anywhere but Deer Park.

"I don't know." Her voice broke, and Maggie pressed her lips together. No way was she going to break down in front of Kane.

"Then take the night to think about it. Get a little sleep, talk to the sheriff again, figure out what all your options are. If you still think you need to run, then do it. But do it smart, not scared." He spoke quietly, not trying to change her mind, simply trying to make her see what she should have before. Running when she was exhausted, hurt and mentally spent wasn't smart, and being smart was the only thing that was going to keep her alive.

"You're right. I need to make some plans."

"If you want help doing it, I'm here." Fabric rustled, and a warm coat settled on Maggie's shoulders. It smelled of icy rain and of Kane, and she didn't know whether she should burrow into it or take it off.

"You're going to freeze," she said as Kane stepped in front of her and tugged the coat closed. His knuckles brushed her collar bone, and Maggie shivered in response.

"Based on the way you're shivering, I think you need the coat more than I do." Hospital lights spilled onto his hair and face, casting shadows and deepening the hard angles of his jaw and cheekbones. He looked mysterious and compelling. A hero come to life, offering his coat and his protection. At that moment, Maggie wanted to believe she could accept them and not regret it later.

"Kane—"

"Come on. Let's get in the car before we both turn to icicles." He led her through the quiet parking garage, his hand on her wrist, his touch light and gentle. He was the kind of guy she'd once dreamed of meeting, the kind who would offer a coat or a ride or a smile.

All she'd met were guys who'd offered nothing but lies and who'd known nothing about family, sacrifice or love.

She shivered again, pulling the coat even closer, allowing herself to enjoy its warmth for just that moment. Tomorrow would be a new day. She'd have to make decisions, act on them, but for tonight, she'd simply pretend that she really was Maggie Tennyson—student, teacher's aide, law-abiding citizen. A woman without a past, without mistakes that haunted her.

"Here we are." Kane opened the door to the SUV, waited while Maggie got inside and then rounded the car to join her. "Are we headed to your country house or to your apartment?"

Maggie hesitated. There was no way she wanted to return to her house, but she didn't want to bring danger to Edith, either. "I'm not sure."

"Your house is isolated. I'd hate to think of you out there by yourself."

"And I'd hate for the guy who shot me to show up on Edith's doorstep."

"How about I call the sheriff and see if he's willing to have a patrol car stationed outside her house for the night? If he can't, you can always stay at the hotel with me and my family."

"And give the reporters something to speculate about? I'd rather take my chances at my place."

"Really?"

"No." She sighed. The day was definitely not going the

way she'd hoped. "Go ahead and call the sheriff. If he can't manage the patrol car, I'll go to the hotel, but I'm not staying with your family."

She leaned her head against the seat as Kane called the sheriff's office, wishing she could go back to the harvest party and keep from being photographed. She'd been so careful for so long, but Deer Park felt like home, and she'd let her guard down. Allowed herself to believe that the past was truly behind her.

That had been her first mistake.

She couldn't afford to make any more.

"Okay. We're set. A sheriff's deputy will park outside Edith's house for the night." Kane broke into her thoughts, and Maggie straightened.

"Thank you."

"All I did was make a phone call."

"You also came to the hospital to make sure I was all right, and you're giving me a ride home."

"That's nothing compared—"

"Let's not. Compare, I mean. I helped Eli because it was the right thing to do. I don't want or need to be repaid."

"Who said anything about repaying?"

"You did earlier. Besides, why else would you be here?"

"I heard you'd been hurt and wanted to make sure you were okay. Isn't that reason enough?" He pulled out into the road, its slick surface shining in the headlights.

"Yes." But she wasn't sure it was. Her life was too complicated already. She didn't need to add a man like Kane into the mix.

"You don't sound convinced."

"I already told you, I don't want any part of the media blitz that's going on in town."

"Would you rather I bring you back to the hospital? You

can call someone else to come give you a ride. Maybe a family member or a friend."

"My friends are all sound asleep, and I don't have any family around."

"You didn't grow up here?"

"I grew up in Florida."

"Yeah? What part?"

"Mia—" Maggie frowned. "Are you interrogating me?"

"I prefer to think of it as an interview." He offered a brief smile, and Maggie frowned.

"An interview for what?"

"I can't help you if I don't know what kind of trouble you're in." He pulled up in front of Edith's house, flashing his headlights at a police cruiser parked on the street a few yards away.

"The police are helping me, Kane. All you should be doing is helping your son."

"I'm capable of doing more than one thing at a time."

"I—"

"It's late. We're both exhausted. How about we save the argument for another day."

He was right, of course. Spending time discussing all the reasons why he shouldn't get involved in her troubles wasn't going to do either of them any good. She pushed the door open and hopped out of the car, grabbing her duffel and offering Kane a smile that felt stiff. "Thanks for the ride."

"Anytime." He followed her out of the car and up to Edith's front door, waiting as she dug the keys from her duffel.

"Good night." She started to open the door, but he put a hand on her arm, holding her in place.

"The deputy I spoke to seemed to think you might have some idea of who shot you tonight."

She wanted to ignore the comment or to pretend she didn't know what he was talking about, but neither would change the truth. "I've got a past, Kane. It's not one I'm proud of, and it isn't one I talk about. It's possible it's finally caught up with me."

"I don't suppose you want to explain."

"I explained to the sheriff. He knows everything he needs to." And it hadn't been easy telling him. Her past wasn't something she liked to talk about. She'd made money the easiest way she could and spent it on drugs and parties. That had been her downfall, but it had also led to her redemption.

She opened the door and stepped into the dark foyer, turning to offer Kane what she hoped was a relaxed smile. "Thank you again for the ride."

"Maggie—"

"My past isn't open for discussion."

"What about your plans?"

"Plans?"

"Are you going to stay in Deer Park or run?"

"I haven't decided."

"Let me know one way or another, okay?"

"Why?"

"Because Eli will want to know if you leave town and because I'll want to know that you've come up with a plan that will keep you safe."

"I'll let you know. Now, if you don't mind, it's late."

"Right. Be safe, Maggie," he said, offering a quick wave as he turned away.

Maggie closed the door and walked up the stairs to her apartment, Kane's words ringing through her head.

Be safe.

If only she knew the best way to do that. Stay. Go. Neither seemed like the perfect plan.

She sighed, dropping onto the sofa and rubbing at the tension in her neck. The house creaked and groaned as the wind buffeted the windows and sprayed ice against the glass. Maggie wanted to pray, wanted to turn her heart and mind to God, but each sound sent her pulse racing, and she could do nothing but sit and listen as the storm raged.

Frustrated, she flipped on the TV, grabbed the afghan from the back of the sofa and wrapped herself in it. The sound of a late-night talk show masked the creaking groan of the house, but it couldn't mask her chaotic thoughts. They were a backdrop to the television and the storm, their iron hold never easing even as Maggie drifted to sleep.

SIX

Thanksgiving.

A day of celebration and thanks.

This one more so than any in the past five years.

Kane knew he should be enjoying it. His parents had arrived with gifts for Eli. A local restaurant had prepared and delivered a Thanksgiving feast, and the hotel had set up a table and chairs in the suite. Now the family was sitting around with plates full of food, eating and talking. All except for Eli. He sat next to Kane, pushing a glob of potatoes around on his plate, silent and frowning.

"Something wrong with the food, buddy?" Kane asked, hoping to elicit some sort of response.

Eli shrugged and scooped the potatoes into his mouth.

"If you don't like the meal, we can get something else. I bet there's a burger place open somewhere around here." Kane's mother, Lila, spoke lightly, but he could hear the concern in her voice.

Kane had tried to warn his parents that Eli had changed. Not that he'd needed to. They understood the trauma their grandson had been through, but knowing it and seeing the product of it were two different things.

"It's okay, Grandma. This is fine." Eli looked up from

his plate of food, offered one of his few smiles, and Kane saw his mother melt.

"You're sure?" she asked, and Eli nodded, looking down again.

"Because I can—"

"He's all right, Mom," Kane cut in, weary from the strain of holding back the emotions that had been pouring through him since he'd heard Eli was alive, weary from two sleepless nights and weary from hours spent trying to find information on Maggie Tennyson. She said she had a past that might be catching up to her.

If someone from that past was trying to harm her, Kane planned to find out who, and he planned to stop him.

Unfortunately, an early-morning Internet search had turned nothing up.

"I don't know about everyone else, but I can't eat another bite. Unless, of course, it's some of that pumpkin pie the hotel sent up." Jenna's voice was overly bright as she carried her plate to the room service cart that stood against the wall. She looked thin. Too thin, and Kane's stomach knotted with concern.

"You should eat a little more, sis."

"And not have room for pie? I don't think so." She shot him a warning look, and he knew exactly what she wanted to say—*Don't you dare give Mom and Dad something else to worry about.*

She was right, of course. The day was emotional enough without adding more to it.

"I'm finished. May I be excused?" Eli spoke into the pause, and Kane was tempted to say that he needed to sit at the table until everyone was finished eating. He didn't. What would be the point? A silent and morose kid at the table wasn't the most joyful way to spend Thanksgiving.

"Sure."

"Can I turn on the television?"

Kane tensed, wishing he could say yes.

Unfortunately, the news about their reunion had been running on every network and cable news program, and he didn't want Eli to watch the coverage unsupervised. "Sorry, buddy. Not right now."

"Then I guess I'll go study my multiplication facts."

"Study on Thanksgiving weekend? I think we can do something more exciting than that," Kane's father, Richard, said, pushing away from the table and stretching.

"Like what?"

"You ever play chess?"

"No."

"Then I'll teach you."

"You will?"

"Of course I will. You're my grandson, and I've taught every one of my kids and grandkids to play chess. Guess what the best part of that is?"

"What?"

"First game you win against me, I give you twenty bucks."

"Twenty dollars! Really?" Eli's eyes were huge, his pale face pink with excitement.

"Really. Now, you go clear a spot in the bedroom, and I'll go fetch my chess set from my room."

"All right." Eli rushed away, and Richard smiled.

"Works every time."

"What?"

"Chess. Sitting across the board from each other really gets communication flowing."

"Yeah, and offering twenty dollars is good incentive to get a kid playing," Jenna said with a laugh.

"Whatever works. I'm going to get that board. Save me

some pie." Richard stepped out of the room, and Jenna shook her head in amusement.

"Leave it to Dad to go simple."

"Simple but effective. I do remember him breaking out that chess game a lot when I was a teenager."

"Yeah, and he brought it to the hospital when I was going through chemo."

"Fortunately for him, he hasn't used it with me." Lila removed the last of the dishes from the table and wiped it down.

"Have I told you how much I appreciate you and Dad coming?" Kane asked, pulling his mother into a bear hug.

"About as many times as I've told you we wouldn't be anywhere else."

"You were planning to have a big family meal with the rest of the gang."

"And the rest of the gang would have given anything to be here instead. Your sisters and their kids all understood, and they're looking forward to seeing Eli again when he's ready."

"If he's ever ready," Kane murmured, glancing at the open bedroom door.

"He will be. Just—"

"Give it time. I know. I'm going to check on him."

He knocked on the bedroom door before he crossed the threshold and was surprised to see Eli slam the phone back onto its receiver. "I thought you were getting a spot ready for your chess game with Grandpa."

"I did." He gestured to the smoothed bed comforter.

"And then you were going to call a friend?" Or had he been dialing his home number, maybe hoping to speak to the woman who'd been calling herself his mother for five years? Susannah Peyton was a liar and a kidnapper, but she *was* the only mom Eli remembered.

"I wasn't calling a friend."

"But you were calling someone. Want to tell me who?" Kane crossed the room and put a hand on Eli's shoulder, refusing to pull away when Eli stiffened. They had a lot of work to do together, a lot of rebuilding. He had to keep that in mind when he was dealing with his son, but that didn't mean not ever reaching out to make the connection he longed for.

"No."

And as simply as that the line was drawn in the sand. Should Kane back off? Insist?

He wasn't sure, and that irritated him. "How about I guess, then?"

Eli didn't respond, just continued to stare down at the hotel carpet.

"Were you calling…" Kane couldn't say "your mother." That would give Susannah more credence than she deserved. "Susannah?"

Eli stiffened at the name but shook his head.

"Are you sure? Because if you were, it's okay. I understand if you miss her."

"I don't."

"Eli—"

"I. Don't," Eli repeated with more emotion than he'd shown since the reunion.

"So you weren't calling her?"

"No."

"Look, son—"

"I was calling information. I wanted Ms. Tennyson's phone number."

"You were calling Maggie?"

"I was trying to, but her number isn't listed."

"Even if her number was listed, it wouldn't be appropriate for you to call her. She's your teacher, Eli. You can't call her at home any time you want."

"It wasn't going to be any time. It was just going to be this time. I wanted to make sure she was okay."

"I told you she was."

"And Mo…Susannah told me you were dead, but you're not," Eli said matter-of-factly, and Kane had no response to that.

He could tell Eli that he'd never lie to him, but Kane doubted his son would believe it. He could say that Susannah was sick and that her sickness had caused her to do an awful thing, but he didn't think that was something Eli was ready to hear.

"I can't give you any more than my word on this, Eli, but the fact is, Maggie really is okay."

"Do you think she'll be at school Monday when I go back?"

"I'm not sure." He wasn't even sure he wanted his son to go back to school. Home school sounded good. A private tutor. Bars on the windows and bolts on the doors.

"I need to find out. She's supposed to help me with my math assignment."

"I can help you."

"I have to do it at school. We do a math assignment every day, and Ms. Tennyson always helps me."

"Eli…" Kane looked into his son's eyes, saw the confusion and anger and hurt there and reached for the phone. "I'll call her for you."

"You have her number?"

He did and had almost dialed it several times already.

Had she done what he suspected she would—packed up and left? If she had, would he be able to track her down and offer her the protection and support she needed but seemed intent on refusing?

"Yes, and I'll call to see if she's all right. Then you're going to play chess with Grandpa and you're going to stop worrying about Maggie." Kane pulled out a piece of paper the sheriff had given him the previous day and dialed the number written on it. One ring. Two. Kane didn't really expect Maggie to answer and was preparing to hang up when the line clicked.

"Hello?"

"Maggie? It's Kane Dougherty."

"Kane? What's up?" She sounded groggy and half asleep, and he imagined her lying on a couch, her honey-blond hair spilling around her shoulders, her eyes still shadowed with dreams.

"I thought I'd call and see how you were doing."

"Give me a minute to wake up, and I'll let you know," she responded on a yawn, and Kane smiled.

"Sorry. I should have realized you'd be sleeping."

"Why? It's three o'clock on Thanksgiving Day. Most people are feasting with family, not sleeping."

"Most people weren't shot last night."

"*Barely* shot," she responded, and Kane laughed.

"I guess you decided to stick around town for a while longer."

"I haven't been awake long enough to decide anything, but last night I was thinking that sticking around and facing my problems might be better than running from them."

"Glad to hear it."

"Don't be too glad—I haven't made up my mind yet."

"Is she okay?" Eli asked, hovering near Kane's elbow and nearly vibrating with anxiety.

"Tell Eli I'm fine," Maggie responded. "As a matter

of fact, I'll tell him myself if you want to put him on the phone."

"Thanks." Kane handed Eli the phone and tapped his fingers against the wall as Eli began chatting enthusiastically. About school. About math. About the turkey he'd barely touched and the pie he wasn't sure he wanted to eat. About the chess game he planned to win once his grandfather taught him how to play. Chatting about everything and anything, as if he'd bottled up his words during the past few days and desperately needed to pour them out.

Finally, he took a breath and tilted his head to the side, listening intently. "So will you be at school this week?"

He was silent as he listened to her response, and Kane could see the disappointment in his face. "All right. I hope you can come, but I understand if you need to get a little better first. Maybe me and Dad could bring you something to eat in a little while. That will help you feel better. We can, can't we, Dad?"

"You're supposed to play chess with Grandpa."

"The game can wait a couple of hours if the boy has something else he's got to do." Richard walked into the room and set a chess set on the bed.

"Thank you, Grandpa," Eli said, offering the same sweet smile he'd offered Lila. "You want us to come, right, Ms. Tennyson? Okay. I'll tell him. Bye."

Eli hung up the phone without giving Kane a chance to speak with Maggie again.

"Ms. Tennyson said it's up to you whether we bring her some Thanksgiving food, but you want to, don't you?"

"Well…" Kane looked into his son's eyes and didn't have the heart to say no. Besides, visiting Maggie might give Kane a chance to get more information about her life before Deer Park. Once he had that, he'd be able to stop the guy who was trying to kill her. "Sure."

"Thanks! She said that turkey sounds good and pie sounds even better."

"Everything okay in here?" Jenna peeked into the room, her face pale, her eyes deeply shadowed.

"Ms. Tennyson doesn't have anyone to spend Thanksgiving with," Eli offered before Kane could respond.

"Ms. Tennyson?"

"Maggie." Kane responded, then frowned when Jenna smiled.

"The blonde with beautiful blue eyes? The one you went to visit at the hospital last night? The one you talked about incessantly until four this morning."

"I wouldn't use the word incessantly, but that's the one."

"Well, why don't we have her over for a second Thanksgiving meal?"

"Because she's recovering from a gunshot wound, and I don't think she wants to leave the house."

"We're going to bring her something instead, and then I'm coming back to beat Grandpa at chess." Eli nearly bounced out of the room, and Kane followed, feeling lighter than he had in years. Over the past few minutes, he'd seen a glimmer of the old Eli, had gotten a peek at the little boy he'd been afraid had been lost to him forever.

That gave him hope, and hope, Kane knew, was a valuable commodity.

It took a few minutes to find a container to carry the food in and a few minutes longer to convince his parents that being thanked by two more members of the family wasn't something that Maggie was up to. His mother still insisted on writing a thank-you note on a piece of Eli's notebook paper and tucking it into Eli's back pocket.

The hotel lobby was empty as Kane and Eli made their way toward the entrance. A few cars dotted the parking lot, and the street in front of the hotel was silent. Small-town life was different than the fast-paced New York scene. Quieter. Slower. Kane wasn't sure if he liked it, but for Eli's sake, he'd stick it out for a few months. Maybe even longer. Whatever it took to help his son heal, that was Kane's new motto. If that meant moving his P.I. firm to Deer Park, Washington, that's exactly what he planned to do.

"In you go, buddy." He opened the car door and waited as Eli climbed in. Then he closed the door and rounded the car.

A shadow moved in his periphery, a subtle shifting that made him tense. He turned quickly, trying to catch sight of whatever had caught his attention. There was nothing, but Kane couldn't shake the feeling that something or someone had been there.

It crawled up his spine, made the hair on the back of his neck stand on end as he got in the SUV. Maybe he should search, see if there really was someone watching, but that would mean leaving Eli alone in the car, and that was something he wasn't willing to do.

He pulled onto the road, glancing in his rearview mirror to make sure he wasn't being followed. The road was still empty—whatever he'd seen in the parking lot was gone.

Which made perfect sense.

Kane and Eli were a curiosity to the people of Deer Park, and anyone could have been staring at them as they made their way across the parking lot. More than one person probably had been.

So why had it felt different than the other times when Kane had caught people looking and pointing as he and Eli walked by?

Why had the shadowy movement felt sinister?

Why was Kane *still* glancing into his rearview mirror, making sure the road remained empty?

And why did he have a feeling that whatever he'd seen was a harbinger of worse to come? A warning that Eli was as vulnerable as he'd been five years ago and just as easily lost?

Kane frowned, flipping on the radio and trying to force the unpleasant thoughts from his mind. Eli was safe. There was no reason to believe otherwise.

No reason, but he couldn't shake the feeling that danger lurked nearby. That one minute of inattention, one moment of carelessness, and the dream could turn into a nightmare again.

His hands tightened around the steering wheel, and he forced himself to relax. To let go of the uneasiness that had settled in the pit of his stomach. God was in control. He'd brought Eli home, and He wouldn't take him away again. Kane believed that. He had to or he'd lock himself and his son in a house somewhere and never come out.

Or he'd run like Maggie once had.

Like she might do again.

Who was after her?

Why?

They were questions he'd been asking since he'd given her a ride home from the hospital, and they were questions he planned to find answers to.

Hopefully soon, because Kane had a feeling that the danger stalking Maggie was going to strike again, and when it did, she might end up with more than a bullet in the shoulder. She might end up dead.

SEVEN

She had to leave.

Sticking close to friends and people who cared had seemed like a good idea when she'd just woken up from a deep sleep, had heard Kane's calm voice in her ear and had allowed herself to think everything was going to be all right. After being awake for an hour, Maggie was thinking more clearly, and what she was thinking was that sticking around Deer Park was going to get her killed.

She tossed several sweaters into her suitcase, dropped jeans on top of the pile and hurried to the closet. There wasn't much she was worried about keeping. Not much that meant enough to bring to whatever new town she landed in. The box was one thing, though, that she wouldn't leave behind. She grabbed it from the top shelf of the closet, upending a pile of blankets and sheets that lay on top of it.

Her shoulder throbbed as she scooped them up, threw them into a pile on the bed and carefully set the box down. She was tempted to open it, to look at the few photos she had of her grandmother and mother, to stare into their lined faces, look into their blank eyes. See what she might have become if she hadn't watched her mother die and made the decision to turn her life around.

She'd made a lot of poor choices in her life. That was true. But there was another truth. God had used Maggie's poor decisions, used the dark times in her life, to bring her close to Him. Derrick was a prime example of that. When Maggie had fled Miami to escape him, desperation had done what years of hard partying could not. It had forced her to reassess her life, to take a look at where she'd been heading and to realize that was not where she really wanted to go. She'd put her troubles and worries in God's hands, and He'd led her to Deer Park. Now He was leading her somewhere new.

And she wanted to accept that. To trust in it.

But she couldn't, because when she thought of leaving all she felt was emptiness.

The phone rang as she shoved T-shirts into the suitcase, but she ignored it. The last thing she wanted was another conversation with Kane, another heart-jerking discussion with Eli. She'd heard the anxiety in Eli's voice, the worry in his father's when she'd spoken to them. The period of adjustment wasn't easy on either, and she'd found herself wanting to make promises to Eli, wanting to assure him that she would be at school when he returned, that she'd be there to help with his math, to talk to him during recess, to offer the stability and familiarity he craved.

She sighed as she grabbed her Bible from the nightstand and set it and the box on top of the T-shirts in her suitcase. She zipped the bulging bag and dragged it into the living room, telling herself that she was *not* abandoning Eli. He had a father, grandparents, people who loved him. He didn't need her, and she didn't need to feel guilty about leaving him.

So why did she?

Because when she looked into his eyes, she saw herself at the same age. A little shy, a little scared, a little unsure, desperately wanting an adult to point her in the right direction and help her make the kind of decisions that wouldn't lead her into the life her mother and grandmother had led.

"But Eli has that. He just doesn't know it yet. So stop feeling guilty, find someone to give you a ride out to your car, and get out of town while you still can," Maggie muttered as she hurried to the kitchen, opened the freezer, reached into the ice cube bin and pulled out two plastic-wrapped wads of cash. She'd learned the trick from Derrick, one of the few things she'd actually found useful.

A sharp knock sounded at the door of her attic apartment as Maggie shoved the money into her purse, and she froze, her heart beating at a sickening pace as she imagined Derrick standing outside the door, waiting for her to open it.

"It's not Derrick. He's too smart to barge into Edith's house when she's got a bunch of guests for Thanksgiving," she mumbled, trying to convince herself that it was true.

The knock sounded again, and Maggie jumped.

It was Edith. Or Kane and Eli, though she doubted they were her visitors.

She hesitated, her hand on the doorknob, her pulse still racing. "Who's there?"

"Kane and Eli. We brought you a Thanksgiving feast."

Her heart jumped in response, her stomach twisting in knots that were half anticipation and half anxiety.

Tell them to go away. Tell them you're not up to visitors.

She should.

Maggie knew it, but she *had* told Eli she was hungry. Had told him that a turkey dinner sounded great. She'd very nearly invited him to bring one over, telling him that it was up to Kane whether or not they delivered Thanksgiving dinner to her house.

What had she been thinking?

Certainly not that Kane would agree to leave his parents and sister to bring the meal.

Or had she?

Kane had made it clear that he owed her a debt of gratitude. He'd gone as far as to call Maggie family.

Why wouldn't he bring her something to eat?

Which brought her right back to where she'd begun— *what had she been thinking?*

"Maggie?" There was a note of concern in Kane's voice, and she wondered if he'd go away if she kept silent long enough.

More likely, he'd break the door down to make sure she wasn't passed out on the floor.

"Just a second." She glanced at the suitcase and decided she didn't have time to drag it back into the bedroom. Not that it mattered. Kane knew she might be leaving Deer Park, and she hoped he wouldn't try to talk her out of it.

She unbolted and unlocked the door and pulled it open.

"Hi. Come on in. Sorry about the mess. I wasn't expecting company."

"If this is a mess, then I'd like to see your version of neat," Kane responded as he and Eli stepped into the apartment. He scanned the room, his gaze touching the couch and the pillow and blankets that lay there, the suitcase sitting near the hall, Maggie's purse on the rickety table and the plastic bags peeking out of it.

Could he see what was in them?

Just the thought made Maggie's cheeks heat, and she scooped up the blankets and pillow and tossed them on top of the purse. Then she gestured to the couch. "Go ahead and have a seat."

Kane raised an eyebrow but didn't comment.

"Here, Ms. Tennyson. This is for you." Eli held out a large plastic container. "My aunt had all her medicine in it, but we washed it out real good before we put the food inside."

"Oh, well, thank you. Is your aunt sick?" Maggie accepted the container.

"She had cancer, but is in remission now," Kane responded, his dark-green eyes staring into Maggie's, asking questions she had no intention of answering. "The medicine is mostly vitamin supplements and herbals that she takes. All boxed and bottled, so don't worry that the food was contaminated with it."

She looked away, walking to the kitchen. "I'm sorry she was so sick, but glad to hear she's in remission. I'll just put the food into another container and wash this out so you can take it back to her."

"Let me." Kane followed her into the kitchen and slipped the container out of her hand. "Where are your plates?"

"Right over the sink, but I can take care of it myself."

"Sure you can, but I'm here, and I don't mind helping." He smiled as he pulled a dinner plate from the cupboard, and Maggie's pulse kicked up a notch.

"Kane, I really…"

"What?" He looked up from the plate he was covering with plastic wrap.

There was no sense telling him she didn't want the help. In a few minutes, he and Eli would be gone, and she'd be on her way to a new life that didn't include either of them. "Never mind."

"I saw the suitcase in the hall. I guess you changed your mind about staying."

"Are you going somewhere, Ms. Tennyson?" Eli hovered just a few feet away, watching her with the same wary look he'd had his first day of school. Poor kid. Caught between two lives, two worlds, and trying to figure out where he really fit in.

That was something Maggie understood, something that resonated with her. Her old life and her new life could not coexist. To survive, she'd have to give them both up. She prayed that wouldn't be true of Eli.

She put a hand on his cheek, forcing a smile she didn't feel. "I'm going on a road trip while I recuperate from my injury."

"Will you be gone long?"

"I don't know."

"You're not coming back, are you?"

She didn't want to lie, but she didn't have the heart to tell him the truth. "A road trip is just that…a trip. Now, come sit down on the couch and tell me all about your Thanksgiving. Did you eat a lot?"

Eli didn't look convinced, but he followed her into the living room and perched on the edge of the couch. "No. I wasn't very hungry."

"Not hungry on Thanksgiving? How can that be?"

"The food wasn't the same."

"No?"

"We usually don't have turkey. We eat chicken. Mom doesn't like turkey." He must have realized what he'd said seconds after the words came out. He blushed, his cheeks going bright pink, his gaze darting to Kane, who seemed to be completely focused on the plastic container he was washing in the sink.

He wasn't oblivious to the conversation, though. His movements were short and tight as he ran the soapy bowl under water again and again.

Poor guy.

It couldn't be easy for him to hear the woman who'd kidnapped his son referred to as Mom.

"Do you like turkey?" she asked Eli, hoping to move the conversation to more neutral territory.

"No."

"Then maybe next year your dad can make turkey and chicken."

"I guess." Eli's response wasn't enthusiastic, and Maggie scrambled for something else to say. Something that wouldn't touch on the fact that Eli's life had been turned upside down.

"Are you going back to school Monday?"

"Dad said maybe, but I don't know if I want to."

"Why not?"

"You're not going to be there."

"Eli…" But there was nothing she could say that would make him feel better, nothing she could do that would ease her guilt. "You'll be fine there without me."

"I guess," he responded, glancing at his father again. "Are you having a good break, Ms. Tennyson? Besides what happened last night, I mean."

"I am now. Thanksgiving turkey and good friends are always a great way to spend the holiday." She offered a smile and was pleased when Eli returned it.

She reached out and pulled him into a hug. It wasn't something she would normally have done, but normally she wasn't leaving for good. Normally she wasn't saying goodbye forever.

She backed off almost immediately and saw that Kane was watching. "Sorry about that. Eli is just such a sweet kid."

"No need to apologize. I'm sure Eli appreciated the hug, didn't you, buddy?"

Eli nodded but didn't speak again. Just stood and moved a few steps closer to the door.

"I guess it's time to get out of your hair," Kane said, his gaze on his son, a frown furrowing his brow.

"I appreciate you coming by and bringing me something to eat."

"It was no problem. Although you may have some explaining to do with your landlady. When she let us in she said you'd told her you were in too much pain to eat."

"I was when she asked if I wanted to join her family celebration."

"I see." He glanced at Maggie's suitcase. "Do you have a ride out of town?"

"Not yet. I'm going to call Adam and see if he'll tow my Ford here. It's still at my house." The house that she was going to abandon. The one she prayed would go to a family that would love it as much as she did.

"Why don't I give you a ride instead?"

"It's better if we say goodbye now," she responded, glancing at Eli.

"For who?" Kane's question speared her heart, and she felt like a coward, running from a little boy who obviously needed her in his life.

"It'll be fun to go for a ride before you leave, Ms. Tennyson. Don't you think?" Eli asked, and she didn't have the heart to refuse.

"Of course."

"Great. I'll get your bag. Is there anything else you need to bring?" Kane grabbed the handle of the suitcase.

"No." She might have said more, but her throat was clogged with tears she refused to shed.

"What about the turkey we brought you. Don't you want it?" Eli asked, and Maggie nodded mutely, hurrying into the kitchen and grabbing the plate of food.

"Can you carry this down for me?" She handed it to Eli, and he beamed with pride as he accepted the assignment.

"Sure."

"Thanks." She shrugged into her coat, wincing as her shoulder protested the sudden movement. Then she grabbed her purse and shoved the plastic bags of cash as far into it as she could.

Kane watched from the doorway, his expression unreadable.

"All set," she said brightly, stepping out into the hall.

The sound of people laughing and talking drifted up the stairs. Edith's family get-together was in full swing, the raucous cheers coming from the living room echoing a sport's announcer's frantic play-by-play.

Maggie had barely stepped down the last stair when Edith peered out of the living room, her shrewd gaze taking in the suitcase, the father and son, and Maggie wearing a coat and ready to run.

"Maggie, what in the world are you doing?"

"Kane is going to take me over to the house to get my car."

"And you need a suitcase to do that?"

"I'm going away for a few days."

"You didn't mention that earlier."

"I just made the decision."

"I'm not sure that's a good idea. You're injured. You should be in bed recovering. Not gallivanting all over creation."

"I won't be gallivanting. I'll be driving," Maggie responded.

"You know what I mean."

"I know, and I'll be fine."

"You'll be back on Monday?"

Maggie hesitated. "I haven't decided yet, but I'll call you once I'm sure of my plans."

She'd call but only to explain that she wasn't coming back.

That thought brought a fresh wave of guilt and regret, and Maggie swallowed the lump in her throat.

"I still don't like this. You've been here for three years, and you've never once gone on an overnight trip."

"There's a first time for everything, I guess." Maggie sidled past Kane and stepped out onto the porch. The air was cold and crisp, the sky overcast. Rain hung in the air, and Maggie breathed in the moisture and tried to memorize the feel of fall in eastern Washington. The thick clouds and tall pines, the scent of earth and evergreen.

"You be careful, you hear?" Edith said, following Maggie onto the porch.

"I will." She wanted to hug Edith and tell her how much she'd miss her, but she didn't dare. Now wasn't the time for explanations. Those would come after Maggie had put some distance between herself and town. "You'd better get back inside before your guests come looking."

"You're right about that. Family is more demanding than any friends I've ever had. See you in a couple of days." Edith hurried back inside.

"Ready?" Kane asked as he carried the suitcase outside, and Maggie nodded, following him to the SUV.

Eli climbed into the vehicle, and Kane shoved the suitcase into the back.

And it was time to leave. Time to say goodbye to the dream she'd been building for three years. Time to say goodbye to the little boy who'd touched her heart and the man who might have found a place in it if she'd given him a chance.

Maggie rounded the SUV as Kane opened the door for her.

He met her eyes and looked like he was about to say something. Then his gaze shifted, settling on a point beyond Maggie's shoulder. His expression changed, his eyes hardening as he lunged toward her and shoved her sideways.

And the world exploded.

She screamed, Kane's forward momentum carrying them both to the ground. Bits of pavement flew into her face and nicked her skin as she fell, and Maggie screamed again.

"*Shhhhh.* I want to hear him if he's coming." Kane pressed her down, keeping her from doing what she wanted. Jumping up, running.

"Dad!" Eli called out, and Kane tensed.

"Stay down, Eli!" he shouted, and Maggie could feel the frantic thud of his heart, hear the hard, quick rasp of his breath.

"Stay here." This time he was talking to her, his lips brushing her ear as he spoke. He levered up and eased to the corner of the SUV. Maggie started to move with him, but he shot her a look that froze her in her tracks.

"Stay there!" he hissed, and Maggie could hear the fear in his voice, the anger.

"Kane—"

But he'd slipped around the side of the SUV and disappeared from view.

And Maggie was left alone, lying on the ground, her ears ringing in the sudden silence.

She eased up, glancing into the window of the SUV. Eli had dropped down onto the floor, waiting there just as his father had told him to. Maggie needed to put some distance between them, make sure that if more bullets flew they wouldn't explode through the car and hit Eli.

She scrambled away, running across the street, hoping to lead her attacker away from Eli, away from Edith's house.

Please, God, please don't let Eli or Kane or Edith be hurt because of me.

A shot rang out, and Maggie dove for cover, rolling behind a pine tree. Someone shouted, the sound carrying through the cold, moist air. Another voice joined the first, this time calling to her.

"Maggie! Get Eli. Take him into the house." Kane panted the words, and Maggie whirled around, searching for him, finding him a few feet from Edith's house, crouched over a man half-hidden by thick shrubs.

Did he have black hair? Black eyes? The slim, muscular build that Maggie had once found so attractive?

She didn't have time to look.

Didn't have time to think about what it would mean if Derrick really were lying on the ground beneath that shrub.

All she could do was run for the SUV, grab Eli by the hand and race into the house.

EIGHT

A kid.

Maybe eighteen or nineteen.

Cheeks pockmarked and sallow from drug use.

That's who had been shooting at Maggie.

Kane wasn't sure who he'd been expecting, but it wasn't the boy cowering at his feet.

"What's your name, kid?" he growled, barely managing to rein in his anger.

"I want a lawyer."

"Strange name. Maybe you should try again." Kane reached down and grabbed the boy's arm, yanking him up and around in one quick motion. He had the kid's arm pinned behind his back and was applying pressure when he heard the first siren. Help was on the way.

Good.

Left too long with the druggy kid, Kane might have given in to temptation and done something he'd regret. Eventually.

"Ow! You're gonna break my arm, man!"

"You were going to shoot a bunch of innocent people. A broken arm is a small price to pay for a crime like that."

"Police brutality. That's what this is."

"Hard for it to be that when I'm not the police." Kane increased the pressure just enough to worry the kid.

"I said, *you're gonna break my arm*."

"Not if you tell me your name and why you were trying to kill my friend."

"Justin."

"And you were trying to kill Maggie because…?"

"I didn't try to kill anyone."

"Right. You were just holding the gun for the fun of it."

"Who said I had a gun?" The kid had obviously gotten some of his fight back, and he tugged against Kane's hold. Or maybe the sound of approaching police cars was giving him a little incentive to try to escape. Either way, he wasn't going to succeed.

Kane tightened his grip and shoved the kid toward the street. "I do. And so will the police once they check the fingerprints on the weapon against yours. So, how about you make things easy on yourself and cooperate?"

"I wasn't coming after you, man. Or the kid. So let me go. Let me go and I'll disappear and you'll never see me again."

"So the only one you were hoping to kill was my friend?"

"I'm not saying nothing."

"You already did," Kane muttered, and the kid tried to pull out of his hold again.

"Look, I wasn't trying to kill no one. I just wanted to scare her. That's all."

"Why?"

"She saw me out at her house. I didn't want her telling the police."

"You're saying you shot her to keep her quiet but you weren't successful, so you came here to finish the job?"

"It was an accident. I didn't mean to shoot her."

"Right." Kane clenched his fist to keep from turning the kid around and *accidentally* punching him in the face.

"It was, man. It really was," he responded, nearly shouting as a police cruiser pulled up and a deputy hopped out.

"What's going on here, folks?"

"I was minding my own business—"

Kane hiked the kid's arm up so high he squealed. "What the kid is trying to say is that he took a potshot at my friend. The gun is over near the shrubs." He gestured to the place where he'd tackled the gunman to the ground.

"I didn't drop no gun, and I didn't try to shoot no one."

"Justin Randall. Didn't I tell you not to get in any more trouble?" The deputy frowned.

"I didn't do nothing."

"The witness here is saying something different. Spread 'em. Let's see if you've got any weapons on you."

"I don't!"

The deputy ignored his protest, frisking him and pulling a plastic bag of colorful pills from his pocket. "You're probably going to tell me this isn't yours."

"I'm not saying anything. I want a lawyer."

"Fine by me." The deputy read him his Miranda rights, helped him into the backseat of the cruiser and closed the door.

"Not the first time you've arrested him, huh?" Kane asked, and the deputy shook his head.

"Kid has been in trouble for years. You want to show me where the gun is?"

"This way. I tackled him and he dropped it in this area."

"He hurt anyone?"

"Not this time, but he admitted to accidentally shooting Maggie. Seems if that were true, he wouldn't have tried to kill her again today," Kane said, glancing at the house, anxious to finish speaking to the deputy so he could get inside and make sure that Eli and Maggie were all right.

"Well, he won't be trying anymore after this. Between the gun and the drugs, we've got enough to put him away for years." The deputy carefully lifted the gun in a gloved hand, emptied the bullets and placed everything in an evidence bag.

"It's possible he isn't working alone."

"What do you mean?" The deputy looked up from the evidence bag and frowned.

"He doesn't seem like the kind to go to a whole lot of trouble for anything, and he's gone through a lot trying to kill Maggie."

"You could have a point, but he fits with the sheriff's profile of the perp—a druggy looking for easy cash. That's who Sheriff O'Malley said might be responsible, and that's who I've got sitting in the backseat of my cruiser."

"Just because you've got one suspect doesn't mean there aren't others."

"I'll call the sheriff, get him to come out here. We'll question Justin together. Maybe we can get the truth from him."

"Good. I'm going inside to check on my son and Maggie."

"Someone will be in shortly to take your statements."

"Thanks."

The door flew open as Kane stepped onto the porch, and Maggie came outside. "Is everything okay? Are *you* okay?"

"I'm fine, and the guy who shot you is in custody, so it's

been a good day's work." He offered a smile, but Maggie didn't look as relieved as he'd expected.

"What's he look like?"

It seemed a strange question, and Kane took a harder look at Maggie's face. She was understandably tense and scared, but there was a sense of anticipation, a vibrating energy that seemed to hang in the air around her.

"Eighteen or nineteen. Scrawny."

"So, he's a kid?"

"Were you expecting someone else?"

"I…don't know." But she *did* know, and Kane wished she trusted him enough to be honest about it.

"The deputy said the kid's name is Justin Randall. Sound familiar?"

"No."

"Did you say Justin Randall?" Maggie's landlady asked, following Maggie onto the porch. Eli hovered in the doorway, his freckles dark against his too-pale face.

"That's what he said."

"I knew that boy would run into trouble. Good parents, but their son sure went wrong."

"That's a shame," Maggie responded, but she seemed distracted, and Kane wanted to take her to a quiet place and ask her the dozen questions that were floating through his mind.

"Why was he trying to hurt Ms. Tennyson?" Eli asked, his brow furrowed, and Kane took him by the hand and pulled him out onto the porch and into a hug. For once, Eli didn't stiffen and pull away.

"He's a sick person. He probably doesn't even realize what he was doing." Kane forced himself to loosen his grip, to let Eli back away.

"Sick like a cold? Or sick in the head?" Eli's question

was so unexpected that Kane laughed, some of his tension and frustration easing.

"Sick like he's addicted to drugs. That can ruin a person's mind."

"Oh. Well, I'm glad he's going to jail. Ms. Tennyson is a nice person, and no one should ever try to hurt her." Eli's earnest response made Maggie smile, and Kane found himself smiling with her. She looked lovely, her hair pulled back into a ponytail, her cheekbones high and sharp. If he didn't know she hadn't been born in Deer Park, he would have thought she was a small-town girl who had just been in the wrong place at the wrong time.

But he did know better, and he wasn't going to make the mistake of believing that Justin going to jail meant Maggie would be safe.

As if she sensed his thoughts, her smile faltered, her gaze jumping from his to the street. "Looks like the sheriff is here."

She was right. The sheriff's car pulled up in front of the house, parking behind the deputy's cruiser.

"Guess we should bring our party back inside. We have pie and ice cream. Want to come in and have some while your dad talks to the sheriff, Eli?" Edith smiled, holding out a hand that Kane knew his son wouldn't take.

"I'd rather stay out here with Dad and Maggie."

"Are you sure? Edith makes a mean pumpkin pie," Maggie said, turning back to face the street and watching as the sheriff approached.

"Pumpkin pie might be good, buddy," Kane said. "Especially since you didn't eat much dinner."

"I like apple pie better," Eli responded with just a touch of rebellion in his voice. Obviously, he didn't want to go inside. Kane was tempted to let him stay, but knew that a discussion about attempted murder and drug addiction wasn't something a nine-year-old should be privy to.

"Then it's good I have apple pie, too," Edith said before Kane could decide what he wanted to say.

"Go ahead, buddy." Kane patted Eli's head and sighed when his son ducked away and hurried into the house.

"It'll get easier," Maggie said, her hand touching Kane's for a second before dropping away. He felt the touch to his core, the heat of it a surprise that stole his thoughts, made him forget that the sheriff was walking up the porch steps, forget that Maggie had secrets she wasn't willing to share. Forget everything but the woman who stood so close he could see the flecks of gold in her blue eyes.

She blinked and took a step back, her eyes wide with surprise, her hand brushing against her jeans as if she could wipe away what they had both felt.

"Howdy, folks. Heard we had some more trouble," the sheriff called out, breaking the tension that hung in the air.

"I'm afraid so." Maggie turned away from Kane, her cheeks pink with whatever emotion she was feeling.

"At least we've got the guy this time. Hopefully, that'll be the end of your troubles."

"I'm not sure..." Maggie shot a glance in Kane's direction, and he wondered if she wanted him to disappear for a few minutes, so she could tell the sheriff whatever was on her mind.

If so, she was going to be disappointed. Kane had no intention of going anywhere.

"You still think that guy in Miami is after you?"

"I'm worried he could be," she responded, keeping her eyes on the sheriff.

"I'll talk to Justin, see what his story is, and I've already spoken to the police in Miami. Your ex is exactly where he's supposed to be."

Her ex? Maggie had been married? Or was it an ex-boyfriend?

"That doesn't mean he didn't pick up a phone and arrange for Justin to try to kill me."

"I'm not saying it does, Maggie. I'm just staying that three years is a long time, and it's very possible your ex has completely forgotten about you."

"It's possible."

But it was obvious from Maggie's tone of voice that she didn't think it was probable.

"Like I said, I'll talk to Justin. See what he has to say. For now, I think we can work under the assumption that he was looking for cash to make another drug deal and things got out of hand."

"Shooting a person is a little more than letting things get out of hand." Kane broke into the conversation, and Maggie and the sheriff both turned to face him.

"You saw the kid. He's hopped up on pills and not in control of himself. I've been trying to put him away for years because I've been afraid something like this would happen."

"He's never done time?"

"He's been booked on drug possession twice. Done community service and rehab. That wasn't enough to keep him out of trouble. It apparently wasn't enough to keep him out of jail, either." The sheriff pulled out a notebook, asked a few questions about the attack and scribbled Maggie's answers.

"All right. I think that's it for now." The sheriff closed the notebook and shoved the pen into his pocket. "I'll give you a call after Justin and I have a little chat about how he got himself into this mess."

"I appreciate it, Sheriff. I'm anxious to hear what he has to say." Maggie shivered, wrapping her arms around her waist as the sheriff walked away.

"You need to get inside and warm up." Kane put an arm around her shoulders, urging her back toward the door.

"Why? So you can follow Sheriff O'Malley and ask questions about the case without me around to hear you?"

"You know me too well." He grinned down at her and was surprised when she returned the smile.

"I don't know you at all, but I'm glad you were here, Kane."

"Does that mean you might be willing to answer some questions I've got for you?"

"Maybe one day, but not now."

"Mr. Dougherty?" the sheriff called out, interrupting the conversation before Kane could press for more.

"Yes?"

"My deputy said you've already answered his questions. It's probably best if you go back to the hotel before the press decides to show up."

"I've been dealing with the press for a long time, Sheriff. Another run-in won't bother me."

"Maybe not, but it might bother Maggie. I don't think she wants people asking a lot of questions about what is or isn't going on between the two of you."

"Going on? There's nothing going on," Maggie said quickly.

"It won't matter. As soon as reporters see the two of you together, they'll start wondering about both of you. Next thing you know, people will be asking how the two of you met, reporters might start looking into your past..." The sheriff's voice trailed off and he gave Maggie a look that seemed to convey a silent message.

"Thanks for the warning, but it's probably too late to be

worried about that. It's all going to come out eventually, so there is no sense worrying about people finding out," Maggie said.

Finding out what?

"You're probably right about that," the sheriff replied. "Now if you'll both excuse me, I'm going to get Justin back to the office and see what he's got to say for himself."

"Thank you, Sheriff." Maggie ran a hand over her hair, offered Kane a weary smile. "I guess I'm going to postpone my trip for a while."

"Yeah?"

"I want to stick around to hear what Justin has to say. Maybe the sheriff is right. Maybe this doesn't have anything to do with my past."

"Do you really believe that?"

"I want to." But she didn't. Kane could see it in her eyes.

"Who is he, Maggie? Who's the guy you're so afraid of?"

"The biggest mistake of my life." She smiled sadly, her lips trembling. "I was a fool. I thought life was all about the next party and my next fix. Derrick was part of that scene. He had money and looks and all the things that were important to me then."

"You married him?"

"I might have if my mother hadn't died of an overdose. If I hadn't decided that I didn't want to meet the same fate."

"So you changed and he didn't."

"Something like that." She smiled again, took a step away. "You're interviewing me again."

"Only because I care." He took a step closer, cupped her chin in his hand, letting his fingers rest on silky skin.

"Don't." She jerked back, her eyes wide.

"Don't what?"

"Look at me like I'm some delicate flower of a woman who needs to be saved. I'm not. I don't." She brushed a strand of hair from her cheek, took a deep breath. "We'd better get inside. I'm sure Eli and Edith are wondering what's taking so long."

She ran into the house before Kane could respond.

It was for the best.

He wasn't sure what he would have said. The fact was, he didn't see Maggie as a delicate woman who needed saving. He saw her as a woman who deserved the second chance she'd created for herself, and he saw himself as the person who was going to make sure she got it.

He doubted Maggie would want to hear that.

He grabbed her suitcase from the SUV and carried it into the house. The foyer was empty, the hushed conversation drifting from a room to the left a sharp contrast to the laughter and cheers that Kane had heard earlier. He brought the suitcase up to Maggie's apartment, then followed the sound of voices back down the stairs and into a large dining room. Several people looked up as he entered, the questions in their eyes obvious. They'd have to go unanswered. No way did he plan to go into details about what had happened. He'd leave that to Maggie.

Eli sat at the far end of the table, a plate piled high with apple pie and ice cream in front of him. A dab of white decorated the corner of his mouth, and his pale cheeks had a tinge of color. He looked young and cute and not nearly as confused and scared as he had been at the hotel. Maybe that was because Maggie sat beside him, her arm touching Eli's as they talked to each other. Kane couldn't hear what was being said, but Eli smiled, looking up into Maggie's face as if she'd managed to lasso the moon and drag it out of the sky for him.

"There you are," Edith called out, pushing away from the table and hurrying toward him. "Our hero!"

"I'm not that, Edith."

"Of course you are. You saved Maggie from being shot. Maybe even killed."

"Edith, this probably isn't the time to discuss it." Maggie stood and placed her hand on Eli's shoulder.

"You're right. Sit down, Kane. Have some pie."

"I wish I could, but my folks are waiting for me back at the hotel. You ready, buddy?"

Eli nodded and stood. "Thank you for the pie, Ms. Edith."

"You're very welcome."

"Ms. Tennyson, maybe you could—"

"I'm going to rest, Eli. You enjoy Thanksgiving with your family." Maggie broke in gently.

"All right."

"Don't sound so glum. You're going to have a wonderful time playing chess with your grandfather." Maggie smiled and took his hand, walking out into the foyer with him.

Kane followed, the subtle scent of Maggie's perfume drifting in the air. She'd spoken of a sordid past, but none of it showed in her face. Her skin was smooth and clear, her face unlined. Whatever she'd done, whoever she'd been, she'd changed. Turned her life around. Kane wouldn't let that be taken from her.

She met his gaze, smiled. "You really were my hero tonight, Kane."

"And you are ours," he responded, putting a hand on Eli's shoulder. "Stay safe."

"You, too." She opened the door, stood on the threshold, watching as they walked to the car. She looked lonely, her shoulders bowed, her face pale, and Kane was tempted to ask her to come to the hotel, join his family for a few hours.

But she'd said she was going to rest, and she needed that more than she needed a boisterous family who'd shower her with thanks and praise.

He waved, smiling as Eli shouted a loud "Happy Thanksgiving" as he climbed into the SUV. Eli's fear and confusion seemed to be receding. Slowly and subtly, but definitely receding. It was something else to be thankful for, and Kane found himself humming along with the radio as he pulled away from Edith's house and headed back to the hotel.

NINE

"You can't hide in your apartment forever. So get up, get dressed and get to church," Maggie muttered to herself as she slapped the off button on the alarm clock and forced herself out of bed.

She'd spent the past two days locked away from the world, and it was time to face it again. No matter how much she didn't want to.

And she didn't.

What she wanted to do was shove her still-packed suitcase into her car and drive away from her troubles.

Unfortunately, that wouldn't get Derrick thrown in jail where he belonged. The only way to defeat him was to draw him out. To do that, Maggie had to stay exactly where she was.

So she was staying.

And she was going to live her life the way she had for three years, do the things she'd always done. That included attending church.

She took a shower and dressed quickly, choosing a simple black skirt and a long-sleeved button-down shirt. She pulled her hair up into a ponytail, swept blush along her cheeks and dabbed on a tinted lip gloss.

Her shoulder still ached, and she winced as she pulled

on her coat. She hesitated at the door, her hand on the knob. Justin was in jail, and the sheriff had told her Thursday that Derrick was still in Miami. She'd heard nothing different since then, and she had no reason to doubt the sheriff's information. She was safe for now.

At least she *hoped* she was safe.

The house was silent as she stepped out onto the landing and walked down the steps. Edith had probably left for church an hour ago. As the church pianist, she was often the first to arrive and one of the last to leave the building. It seemed today was no different.

Bright sunlight and fresh air lifted Maggie's spirits, and she hummed a tune as she got in the Ford. Soon, the first snow would fall in the mountains, covering their distant peaks with white powder. Whereas Miami had been hot and filled with bright colors and vibrant life, Washington was cool and dry, its pallet of colors muted. Quieter, more subtle and somehow more comforting. It suited Maggie. If any place had ever been home, this was it.

Maybe that's why she was so determined to stay.

Or maybe she was simply tired of running, tired of hiding, tired of wondering if her past were lurking just around the corner, waiting to jump out and snag her again.

She frowned, pulling into the parking lot of Starr Road Christian Church. The building that housed it was as unpretentious as the people who made up the congregation. One-story with weathered wood siding, it had seemed like the kind of church that might be willing to welcome Maggie when she'd arrived in town three years ago. Weary, worn and tarnished, Maggie hadn't felt she'd belonged in the fancy churches she'd visited, but Starr Road had seemed as weary as she was, the building timeworn and comfortable. When she'd stepped inside, she'd felt the warmth of the people, had seen nothing but understanding and acceptance in their eyes. She had returned again and again. Now, the church was her family.

She stepped out of the car and smiled at an elderly couple who were slowly making their way across the parking lot. Several other people were meandering toward the door, and Maggie joined them, talking and smiling and acting for all the world like it was any ordinary Sunday.

"Glad to see you made it today," Judith Blanchard said as she joined the small group. Fifty-something with salt-and-pepper hair and a gruff, sometimes overbearing attitude, Judith was the kind of person who wasn't afraid to share her opinion or her faith. She also wasn't above a little gossiping if she thought what she was saying was in the best interest of the church community.

"Thank you." Maggie kept her reply simple, not wanting to encourage questions or comments about the past week. She knew that news of her ordeal had spread. As a matter of fact, she'd spent most of her two days at home answering phone calls and reassuring people that she was all right.

"I was worried you might still be recovering from that gunshot wound."

"It's much better. Thanks for your concern."

"Heard it was that Justin boy who shot you. Heard he wanted to steal some cash from your place and you fought him off, beat him down and he resented it."

"What?" Surprised, Maggie stopped in her tracks, and the entire group stopped with her. "You're kidding, right?"

"I think you know me well enough to know I'm not much of a kidder. I'm telling you like it was told to me."

"By whom?"

"Cynthia Whitmore. She's does my hair once a month.

She's the only one I trust to perm it." Judith patted her tightly curled hair.

"Well, she's exaggerated the story. I didn't fight Justin off. He took a shot at me outside my house. I ran inside and called the police."

"That's it?"

"That's it."

"Not nearly as exciting as Cynthia made it out to be." Judith scowled, and Maggie couldn't help smiling.

"I knew you had it wrong all along, Judith," Karen Mitford said, her petite figure nearly vibrating with excitement. "It wasn't Maggie who fought off Justin. It was that good-looking Kane Dougherty. The one who's been in the news because of being reunited with his son."

"Now why would Maggie be hanging around with the likes of Kane Dougherty?" Judith huffed, and Karen leaned closer into the group, glancing around as if Maggie weren't standing right there with her, listening to every word.

"The way I hear it, he's got a soft spot for our Maggie."

"Karen, why would you say something like that?" Maggie asked, her cheeks heating.

"Because that's what Mimi Lesnever said. Her husband is a deputy with the sheriff's office, and he was there when Justin tried to kill you the second time. He told Mimi that Kane Dougherty is sweet on you."

"Well, he's wrong," Maggie responded, not nearly as amused as she'd been a few minutes before.

Kane sweet on her?

It was laughable.

So, why wasn't Maggie laughing?

"But Richard Lesnever is a man, dear. And men know these kinds of things about each other. So, if he says Kane Dougherty is—"

"He is *not* sweet on me."

"My! Someone is defensive," Judith cut in, and Maggie wished she'd done what she wanted to and stayed in bed.

"Look, ladies, I know it's fun to speculate about my love life, but since I don't actually have one, how about we talk about something else?"

"Ms. Tennyson!" A young voice called out, and it sounded just like Eli's. Only there was no way Eli could be at church.

Was there?

She turned, scanning the parking lot, and nearly bolted when she saw Eli walking toward her, his father close to his side.

Kane in bright daylight was something to behold. He wore a sports coat, dark slacks and a pale-green dress shirt, and he hadn't bothered with a tie. The top button of the shirt was open, revealing just a hint of tawny skin. He should have looked professional and a little boring, but somehow managed to look Herculean.

And Maggie was sure she heard the group that surrounded her heave a collective sigh.

"Eli! Kane! What are you doing here?" She walked forward to meet them, knowing that every word she said was being heard and judged by some of the nosiest women in the church.

"I called around to find a good church to attend," Kane said. "This is where I ended up."

"You called Edith, didn't you?"

"Guilty as charged." He smiled, and Maggie was surprised none of the ladies noticeably swooned.

"Well, it's good to see you both. You're looking very handsome, Eli."

"I wanted to wear jeans, but Dad wouldn't let me." Eli frowned, shifting uncomfortably in his dress pants and button-up shirt.

"That's okay. You'll fit right in with the rest of the kids."

"I don't think I will. Dad said church was good for us, but I don't think he's right."

"Why not?"

"Because it's boring."

"Have you been before?"

"No."

"Then how do you know it's boring?"

"Because it probably is."

"Eli, we had this conversation back at the hotel, and we agreed we'd give church a try," Kane said calmly, offering Maggie an apologetic smile.

"*You* said we were coming, but I didn't want to. I wanted to stay with Grandma and Grandpa and Aunt Jenna."

"You know Aunt Jenna wasn't feeling well, and Grandma and Grandpa were taking her to the doctor."

"I could have gone with them if you'd let me." Eli's protest didn't have much heat, but it surprised Maggie anyway. In the time she'd known him, Eli had never been anything but cooperative. Shy and sweet, he'd always been eager to please.

"I'm sure that your father didn't want you to hang around a doctor's office for hours."

"They were going to the emergency room. I think that would have been cool. Cooler than church."

"Is your sister okay?" Maggie asked, ignoring Eli's comment and shooting a look in Kane's direction. The last thing the family needed was a serious illness.

"She has a stomach bug, and my parents are concerned that she's dehydrated."

"I'll be praying that she feels better."

"We could all go to the hospital, then we'd *know* she was feeling better," Eli said.

"We're not going to the hospital, Eli." Kane sounded weary.

"But—"

"I used to think church was boring, too," Maggie cut in, hoping to diffuse things.

"You did?" Eli looked at her with his father's eyes, and Maggie's heart melted. He was young and confused and doing everything he could to regain some control over his life.

"Sure. So did my mom and my grandmother. 'Church is for people who've got nothing better to do,' that's what they always said. I thought they were right until I decided to try it one Sunday, then I realized it was for everyone. Even kids like you."

"I still would rather go to the emergency room."

"I'm sure you would, but since you're here, maybe we can sit together. If that's okay with your father."

"I don't have a problem with it. As a matter of fact, Eli and I were hoping to run into you here today. Weren't we, sport?"

This time Maggie was absolutely sure she heard a sigh come from behind her. She glanced over her shoulder and saw that several women were still watching intently.

She speared them with a look she hoped would send them running for the church. Instead, it seemed to amuse them. Their laughter carried across the parking lot as they hurried into the building, and Kane raised an eyebrow.

"Friends of yours?"

"Admirers of yours."

"Yeah?" He put a hand on her lower back, urging her toward the building.

"They saw you on the news and heard the harrowing tale of how you saved me from Justin."

"Probably embellished liberally."

"What's to embellish? You saved my life, and they heard about it and were duly impressed."

"Nice, but there's only one lady here I'm interested in impressing. Want to guess who she is?" He grinned, his eyes flashing with green fire, and Maggie's mouth went dry, her heart skipped a beat and she knew she was in big, big trouble.

"I've never been very good at guessing games."

"I'm good at them, and I guess that he wants to impress you, Ms. Tennyson," Eli said, and Kane's grin broadened.

"The service is starting. We'd better hurry up." No way was she going to acknowledge Kane's question, and no way was she going to think about Eli's response.

The sanctuary was a long room set up with lines of folding chairs. Maggie made her way to three seats and took the one farthest from the aisle, patting the seat beside her as Eli hesitated. "Come on. I don't bite."

"You're not boring, either, but I still think church is going to be." He sat, glancing around the crowded building as Kane took the seat beside him.

"What do we do now?" Eli asked, his question barely carrying over the chatter of the members and visitors.

"We sit for a few minutes. Then Ms. Edith will play piano, and we'll sing a few songs and pray for people who need help. The pastor will say a few things, and then it will be over."

"Oh." Eli frowned, and Maggie knew he was probably thinking that church was going to be just as boring as he'd imagined it would be.

"There's a children's church if you and your father think you should go." Maggie looked at Kane, and he gave a subtle shake of his head.

So, children's church was out.

She searched through her purse, pulled out a pen and handed it to Eli. "Hold on, I'll go get some paper from the children's church room and you can draw some pictures while you listen."

"I don't wa—"

"Eli, Ms. Tennyson is being very patient with you, but *my* patience is wearing thin. Whether or not you want to be here, you are. You may as well make the best of it." Kane spoke with quiet authority, and Eli had the good grace to look contrite.

"I'm sorry," he said, looking at Maggie rather than his father. "I'd like some paper, please."

"I'll be right back." Maggie started to stand, and Kane stood with her, stepping out into the aisle before she could move.

"I'll get it. I'm closer anyway. Just point me in the right direction."

"Out the door and up the hall. Children's church is the second room on the left." She gestured to the door they'd entered, and Kane nodded.

"Okay." But instead of walking away, he stood where he was, studying her intently.

"What?"

"I was just noticing how breathtakingly beautiful you are." He didn't even smile as he said it, and Maggie's cheeks blazed.

"Maybe I should get the paper after all," she said, ready to hurry up the aisle and away from Kane's charm.

"No need to run away, Maggie. Compliments aren't dangerous."

They were when they came from a man like him.

But she wasn't going to tell *Kane* that.

"I'm not running. Church is going to start soon, and if

Eli is going to have something to color on, one of us needs to get the paper."

"Right." This time Kane did smile, and Maggie's heart did a backflip. Twice.

"Look, Kane—"

"I'll get the paper. You're going to stay with Eli while I'm gone, right?"

"Of course." She'd stay even though what she really wanted to do was exactly what Kane had said—run. Back to her apartment and her quiet, orderly life.

"You know what, Ms. Tennyson?" Eli said as she sat down, his green eyes staring straight into hers.

"What?"

"My dad is right."

"About you making the best of things?"

"No. About you being beautiful."

"Oh, Eli, that's so sweet of you to say." She smiled, ruffling his hair and trying to forget how she'd felt when his father had said the same words.

"Do you think my father is handsome?"

Surprised, she took a hard look at Eli. He looked as innocent as a nine-year-old could be, his expression guileless. "Why do you ask?"

"Well, he thinks you're beautiful. If you think he's handsome then maybe you guys could date. Then I could see you more often."

"Your father and I have only known each other a few days. We certainly aren't going to start dating."

"How long do you need to know someone before you do start dating?"

In Maggie's case, a lifetime.

"It depends on the people."

"With you and my dad, how long do you think it will take?"

The first strains of the call to worship interrupted the conversation before Maggie could respond, and she settled into her seat, relieved to have an excuse to end the conversation.

"We have to be quiet now. The service is starting," she whispered.

"Okay." And he sounded so disappointed that Maggie wanted to pull him into a bear hug and tell him that he could see her any time he wanted to.

She didn't, of course.

Instead, she grabbed a hymnal from beneath the chair, stood with the rest of the congregation and urged Eli to do the same. They were on the second stanza when Kane returned. He had paper in one hand and a fistful of crayons in the other, and he set everything on Eli's chair before moving close to Eli and joining in the singing.

Despite the number of voices lifted in praise, Maggie could hear Kane's deep baritone. She glanced his way, saw that he was watching her and felt her cheeks heat again.

What was it about the man that made her feel like an inexperienced schoolgirl?

Whatever it was, she planned to ignore it.

She had enough to worry about, enough to think about without adding Kane into the mix. Staying in Deer Park might be the right thing to do, but she wasn't convinced it would keep her safe. She needed to pay attention to her surroundings, and that would be difficult if she was distracted by a man.

So she wouldn't be. Period. End of story.

No matter how good-looking, charming and brave that man was.

The hymn ended, and Maggie sat down, refusing to look at Kane again, refusing to even think about the fact that he was only two seats away.

She'd come to church to worship, to thank God for the blessing He'd given. She had not come to spend an hour thinking about Kane.

So why are you still thinking about him?

The question flitted through her mind, but she ignored it.

She didn't have time for childish crushes.

A crush?

She refused to even call it that.

What she felt for Kane was nothing more than physical attraction. So what if he was proving himself to be a compassionate and caring father? So what if he seemed to always be around when Maggie needed him? And so what if he'd risked his life to save her?

He was still just a man.

And Maggie had given up on men three years ago.

She wasn't going to forget that. Not for Kane. Not for anyone.

She frowned, opening the hymnal to the second hymn, determined to lose herself in the words and to forget everything else. All her troubles, her past, Derrick. Kane.

Those things were temporary, and they'd fade like the seasons. What would last was her faith, and that was enough to carry her through whatever would come.

TEN

Church hadn't been important to Kane when he'd been a young attorney just starting out in New York. After his marriage to Sophia, he'd attended services sporadically, spurred on by his wife. When she'd died, he'd gone back to his old habit of sleeping in, figuring that Eli was too young to benefit from church.

He'd been wrong, of course, and he'd spent a lot of years regretting it. After all, Kane's childhood had been filled with church activities and church friends. He'd attended camps and youth group meetings. He'd even gone on a mission trip when he was in high school. He had known what faith was, had a firm foundation in the Bible, but he'd never felt he needed God. Until Sophia died. Until Eli disappeared. Until Kane's sorrow had threatened to eat him up from the inside out.

That's when he'd found himself on his knees, crying out to God, begging for a miracle. He hadn't gotten it then, but Kane had finally understood what it meant to need God, and it had humbled him. Since then, church had been a big part of his life. He enjoyed the fellowship, the worship and the feeling that somehow he was connected to something much greater than himself.

Too bad his son didn't feel the same way.

Eli stood beside him, staring down at the hymnal Maggie held, but he was not singing. Kane wanted to tap him on the shoulder and insist that he participate, but what would be the point? It wouldn't mean anything, and it would only put more of a rift between them.

He sighed, and, as they sat, he rubbed the back of his neck and tried to ease some of his tension. Being around Eli was like walking a tightrope. Every step was a study in balance. Too far one way or too far the other might send them both spinning out into freefall.

"Come to Me all you who are weary and heavy laden, and I will give you rest." The pastor's words cut through Kane's thoughts, and he focused his attention on the lanky, fortysomething's message. It was similar to others he'd heard, but this time it struck a deeper chord.

Rest.

That sounded great to Kane. He'd barely slept in the past few days, and in the years preceding those his sleep had often been restless and filled with nightmares. His faith had floundered, his need to know what had happened to Eli, why it had happened, overshadowing everything else.

Rest.

It wasn't an easy thing to find when your mind was filled with worries and your stomach churning with sorrow. That's something Kane had learned in the past five years, something he'd come to accept.

But I want it, Lord. I want that kind of rest. The kind that doesn't depend on circumstances, but depends solely on You, he prayed silently as the sermon ended and the congregation stood for the last hymn.

Maggie handed him a hymnal, her fingers brushing his, the contact sending warmth up his arm. He wanted to grasp her hand, hold it as they sang the final hymn, but he knew she'd pull away.

Dressed in a slim black skirt and a fitted shirt, her hair pulled back into a ponytail, she looked lovely, young and serene. Only the wariness in her eyes gave away the truth of how she felt and what she was thinking.

She must have sensed his scrutiny. She met his gaze, her cheeks turning pink, a frown line marring the smooth skin between her brows.

Obviously, she wasn't as enamored of Kane as he was of her.

Enamored?

Bad choice of words. He wasn't enamored, he was… intrigued by her beauty, her kindness, her obvious faith.

"Is it over, Dad?" Eli whispered, and Kane jerked his attention away from Maggie and back where it belonged.

"One more prayer, and then we're done."

"And then we're going back to the hotel?"

"How about we discuss that after the prayer?"

Eli shrugged, and Kane bit back a sigh.

This seemed to be their pattern. Eli would ask something of Kane that Kane couldn't give and then would fall silent when his wishes weren't granted.

Was being sullen a normal nine-year-old thing, or was the sullenness a product of Eli's deep unhappiness at the situation he'd found himself in? Either way, Kane was worn from it.

As soon as the last prayer ended, Eli tried to sidle past Kane.

Kane grabbed his arm, holding him in place, afraid of losing sight of him in the crowded sanctuary. "Hold on, buddy. There's no rush."

"Sorry," Eli mumbled, holding still while Kane slid the hymnal under a seat and grabbed the papers and crayons Eli had left on the chair.

"There's a side door over this way, if you want to leave

quickly." Maggie's voice carried over the cheerful cacophony of the departing congregation, and she gestured at a door near the front of the sanctuary. The crowd exiting through it was less dense than the one streaming through the middle aisle, and Kane nodded.

"Good idea. Thanks." He kept his hand on Eli's shoulder, following Maggie into the side aisle and trying not to notice the graceful way she moved, the slim curve of her waist, the golden fall of her ponytail.

Tried not to.

But not noticing Maggie was nearly impossible.

"So, what do you think, Eli? Was church boring?" She glanced over her shoulder, offering Eli a sweet smile, and Kane's pulse leaped.

"I guess not."

"So, maybe you'll come again on Wednesday night. We're having a potluck."

"What's that?" Eli asked, shrugging out from under Kane's hand and hurrying forward to match pace with Maggie as she stepped outside.

"Everyone brings something to eat and then we all share it while we talk and get to know each other. There'll be lots of kids there. You know Timothy Briton from class? He'll be there. His mom always brings the best desserts."

"I don't think my dad will let me go," Eli said, as if Kane weren't just a few steps away.

"Why not?" he asked as the pair stopped near Maggie's car.

Both turned to look at him, and Maggie flashed an apologetic smile. "I'm sorry, Kane. I should have thought to ask you before I brought it up to Eli."

"No need to apologize. I think it sounds like a great idea."

"Wonderful. I'll see you both then." She pulled open

the door, hopped into the car and probably would have slammed the door shut again if Eli hadn't been in the way.

"I'm going to be at school on Tuesday. Will you be there, Ms. Tennyson?"

"Unless the doctor tells me I need to stay home and rest my shoulder."

Kane's cell phone rang while Eli began what threatened to be a very long monologue about a book report that was due on Friday.

"Hello?"

"Kane, it's Mom." Lila Dougherty was one of the calmest people Kane knew, so when his mother sounded frazzled or scared, he knew something was seriously wrong.

And that was exactly how she sounded. Frazzled, scared, maybe even a little frantic.

"What's wrong?"

Maggie looked up and Kane could see the questions in her eyes.

"They've decided to admit Jenna. The E.R. doctor is concerned that there might be something more going on than a stomach bug."

"Like what?"

"He wouldn't say, but Jenna is thinking the worst." *And so am I.* The last remained unspoken, but Kane knew it was what his mother was thinking. He was thinking the same. Thinking about Jenna's paleness, her fatigue, the quick way she'd cut him off when he'd tried to ask about her doctor's appointment.

"I'll be there as soon as I can."

"But what about Eli?"

"I'll bring him."

"And have him sit around with a bunch of gloomy, worried people while they wait to find out whether or not his aunt's cancer has returned? Kane, I know you're his father, but…"

"No, you're right, Mom. That's probably not the best idea. I'll go back to the hotel and wait for you to call with more news. Tell Jenna that…tell her I'm praying and that I think everything is going to be just fine."

"I will."

Kane hung up and shoved the phone into his pocket, more alarmed than he wanted to be. Jenna's cancer had nearly killed her, but she'd fought hard and had won.

Or so they'd thought.

Was it possible she was sick again? That the cancer they'd thought she'd beat had returned?

"Is your sister okay?" Maggie got out of the car and held Eli's hand as she faced Kane. They could have been mother and son, the two of them. Both standing with their heads cocked to the side, their bodies tense and their eyes wary.

"They're admitting her. They want to run a few tests." He didn't offer more. There was no sense in giving Eli something else to worry about.

"You want to be there with her."

It was a statement rather than a question, but Kane answered anyway. "I'd like to, but I don't think the hospital is the best place for Eli. Besides, we had plans to have ice-cream sundaes this afternoon, right, bud?"

Eli nodded his agreement, but didn't look any more excited by the idea than he had when Kane had first brought it up.

"If you want…" Maggie bit her lip, and Kane's gaze was drawn to the fullness of her mouth.

"What?"

"Eli and I could go for lunch and ice cream while you go to the hospital."

"I couldn't ask you to do that, Maggie."

"Why not?" Eli asked, and Kane bit back impatience.

"Because Ms. Tennyson has other things to do with her time, Eli."

"Actually, I don't," she offered. "I usually spend my Sundays relaxing, and what could be more relaxing than ice cream and friendship?"

"There are still reporters all over town, Maggie. They stopped short of following us from the hotel this morning when I told them we were going to church and wanted them to respect our privacy while we worshipped, but if they see you and Eli together, they'll be snapping pictures, asking questions, all the things you wanted to avoid."

"Worrying about that now is like worrying about spilling milk when it's already on the floor. It's too late. My photo was in the news, and I can't change it, so I may as well stop worrying about it."

"Are you still afraid your ex is going to come after you?"

"I don't know. He's got a long memory, and whether the sheriff believes me or not, I'm sure that Derr…" Her voice trailed off and she shook her head. "You're right. It's probably best if Eli and I don't go get ice cream. I wouldn't want anything to happen while we were together."

"We could go to your house, Ms. Tennyson. We could have ice cream there."

"We can't put Ms. Tennyson out like that."

"You wouldn't be putting me out. If Eli wants to spend the afternoon at my place, I'm happy to have him if you're okay with it."

Was he?

"Please, Dad?"

Kane hesitated, trying to imagine every worst-case scenario. If Maggie's ex came after her, he didn't want his son anywhere close by.

"No, Eli. I'm sorry, but it's better if we go back to the hotel."

Eli's face fell, and Maggie looked just as disheartened.

"Why don't we all have ice cream together?" he offered, feeling like the worst kind of heel.

"That would defeat the whole purpose, Kane. I was going to have Eli over so that you could be at the hospital with your sister," Maggie said quickly, and Kane had the distinct impression that she'd rather do just about anything but spend time with him.

"But ice cream would still be fun. Wouldn't it, Ms. Tennyson?" Eli looked up at Maggie, and Kane wondered if she'd have the heart to say no.

"Eli…" Maggie hesitated, then sighed. "That sounds good. We'll go back to my place, have some lunch and then have ice cream."

"Thank you!" Eli threw himself into her arms.

She laughed, accepting his hug, and Kane's throat tightened with emotion. Maybe things weren't as dire as they seemed. Maybe Eli did just need some time to adjust because at that moment, he looked a lot like the little boy Kane remembered. Happy, smiling and excited by life.

"You're welcome. So, how about we get going? My stomach is growling." She got in her car, this time managing to close the door quickly.

"Come on, buddy. Let's go."

"I could ride with Ms.—"

"No, you couldn't because I'm your father, and I want to spend time with you." He put a hand on Eli's shoulder and steered him to their SUV.

He expected Eli to go back to his solemn, sullen silence,

but Eli looked Kane in the eye as he climbed into the SUV and offered a shy smile. "I want to spend time with you, too, but you're not who I remember."

"I didn't think you remembered me at all," Kane responded, his heart beating hard against his ribs. He didn't want to say the wrong thing, didn't want to do anything to stop Eli's words from flowing.

"I remember we played catch together. I remember that you used to make pancakes for breakfast."

"Almost every Sunday morning."

"I remember I was sad when Mo—Susannah told me you didn't want me anymore."

"I'm sorry, Eli. I wish things could have been different."

Eli shrugged, buckled his seat belt and turned away, ending the conversation as quickly as he'd started it.

Kane was both relieved and disappointed. Relieved because hearing about Eli's life was like having a knife thrust through his heart. It was almost too painful to bear. Disappointed, because, despite the pain, Kane needed to know what kind of life Eli had been living with Susannah if he were ever going to have a better understanding of his son. So far, Susannah wasn't talking, and, though the FBI had traced much of her movements during the past five years, they couldn't speculate on how she'd treated Eli.

His cell phone rang as he pulled out of the church parking lot, and he answered, expecting it to be his mother or father.

"Hello?"

"Hey, it's Jackson." Jackson Sharo was one of Kane's best investigators. A former New York City homicide detective, he'd joined Kane's P.I. firm after his sister was murdered by her estranged husband and had been part of the Information Unlimited team ever since.

"What's up?"

"That's what I was calling to ask you. I phoned into the office, and Skylar said you'd run into some complications."

"Nothing I can't handle."

"She also said the woman who helped you find Eli was shot," Jackson continued, completely ignoring Kane's response.

"Skylar talks too much." But she was a great investigator. Which was why Kane had asked her to help him find information on Maggie. She'd come up as empty as he had.

"She's concerned."

"She shouldn't be. Things are cool here. How about with you? Did you find your brother-in-law?" Jackson had taken a week off to fly to Cancún with his new wife, Morgan. They were hoping to track down the brother Morgan had been separated from when she was a child. Adopted by different families, Morgan and Nikolai hadn't seen each other in two decades. A reunion between them would mean another blessing for the Information Unlimited team.

"We haven't been able to locate him yet. Seems like every time we show up at his condo, he's just left. At least that's what his neighbor says."

"You think he's hiding from you?"

"I don't know, but I'm not giving up until Morgan gets a chance to see him face-to-face. If he *is* Nikolai, she needs to know. Whether he wants to see her or not."

"Keep me updated."

"How are things going with Eli?"

"As well as can be expected," Kane said, glancing in the rearview mirror. Eli was staring out the window, but that didn't mean he wasn't listening.

"Morgan and I have been praying for the two of you."

"We need it."

"And do you need me? If things are going badly up there, I can fly in for a few days and offer support."

"What kind of support are you thinking I need?"

"More manpower."

"You mean more weapon power."

"That, too."

"I'm good for now. I'll let you know if things change. Now, you'd better get back to searching for Nikolai."

"Take care, boss." Jackson hung up before Kane could tell him to knock off the boss thing.

He shoved the phone back in his pocket as he pulled up in front of Edith's house.

Maggie was standing on the porch, her ponytail falling over her shoulder in a silky gold rope. She looked nervous and uneasy, her shoulders tense, and Kane wondered what it was about him that made her so uneasy.

Was it the fact that he was a private investigator and she had secrets?

Was it the fact that there was obvious chemistry between them?

Or was it simply that Kane was a man, and Maggie had been abused or disappointed or both one too many times in her life?

"Ready to eat?" She smiled brightly as Eli bounded up the stairs, but her nervousness was impossible to hide.

"What are we going to have?"

"How about pizza? That's easy to make and I have all the ingredients."

"We can *make* pizza?"

"Sure. I'll show you how, and then we can play a game while it cooks."

"What kind of game?"

"We'll think of something," Maggie said, unlocking the door and hurrying inside.

She hadn't offered Kane more than a brief glance.

Maybe she wished he'd change his mind and go to the hospital.

He wouldn't.

There was too much at stake. Eli's safety. Maggie's.

Until Kane knew for sure that Maggie's ex wasn't coming after her, he'd make no assumptions and take nothing for granted.

He scanned the empty street, searching for danger but finding nothing. The day was peaceful and silent. Of course, things could change in an instant. He'd learned that the day Eli disappeared, and it wasn't something he'd ever forget.

Help me keep Eli and Maggie safe, Lord, he prayed silently as he followed Maggie and Eli up the stairs and into her apartment.

ELEVEN

Maggie held the bowl of mozzarella cheese as Eli finished sprinkling the contents over their pizza.

"Now what?" he asked as he took the bowl and dumped the last few crumbs onto the pie.

"It's ready to bake. Fifteen minutes and we'll be eating."

"That's not very long." Eli stood back while Maggie opened the oven and slid the pizza in.

"No, it's not."

"But it's enough time to play a game, right?"

"Sure, but we'll have to go downstairs and borrow one from Ms. Edith." Maggie washed her hands, gestured for Eli to do the same, and then stepped out of the kitchen, bracing herself for what she knew she'd see—Kane sitting at the small dining room table, his laptop in front of him as he worked. He'd retrieved it from his SUV when she'd said that her galley kitchen was too small to accommodate more than one helper.

She'd avoided having him under her feet and succeeded in creating the kind of wholesome domestic scene that could have come from any 1950s-era television show. Which was exactly the kind of life she'd wanted when she was Eli's age. She could still remember lying in bed, listening to her mother's hard-partying friends and imagining that she lived in another home with another family. One that cared. She'd been young then and naive enough to think she really could make a better life than the one her mother and grandmother had created.

And she had, eventually.

She wasn't going to mess that up by allowing a man into it.

Kane looked up as she walked into the room, offering a half smile, his green eyes as warm and inviting as the sun after a winter storm.

"You guys finished?" he asked.

"Yes. The pizza will be ready in fifteen minutes. Eli and I are going to go down and borrow a game from Edith."

"I'll come with you. I need to stretch anyway." He stood, and Maggie couldn't help noticing the way his shirt hugged well-built shoulders and muscular biceps, couldn't stop from thinking that having him around brought renewed energy into her tired little apartment.

"I'm ready. Can we go get the game now?" Eli walked out of the kitchen, and Maggie turned away from Kane, glad for the distraction and determined to ignore the man as much as possible for the next few hours. If she didn't, she might find herself sinking way deeper into a relationship with him than she wanted to.

"Sure. Ms. Edith has dozens. She says they're for her grandkids, but I think she likes to play, too."

"I hope she has Monopoly."

"You like playing Monopoly? That's always been one of my favorites," Kane said as he followed them out into the hall.

Did he feel like a third wheel, an outsider trying his best to become one of the gang?

The thought made Maggie rethink her plan to ignore

him. Doing so wasn't fair to Kane, it wasn't fair to Eli and it probably wasn't even fair to Maggie. She was, after all, a grown woman. Completely capable of having a man in her home, in her life without falling for him.

She hoped.

"I was always more of a trivia nut, but I'm game for a round of Monopoly if you guys are," she said, hoping Kane couldn't hear the uneasiness in her voice.

"Did I hear someone mention Monopoly?" Edith asked, peeking her head out of her living room.

"We were going to borrow the game from you, Ms. Edith," Eli responded. "Me and Ms. Tennyson made pizza, and we're going to start the game while we wait for it to cook."

"Pizza and Monopoly. Now that does sound like a load of fun. I don't suppose you all have room for one more?"

Maggie nearly jumped with relief at the thought of Edith joining the game. At least with another adult around, things wouldn't feel quite so comfortably domestic.

"That sounds good to me. What do you think, Eli? Kane?"

"Works for me," Kane responded, and Eli nodded a slightly less enthusiastic agreement.

"We can set the game up on my kitchen table and eat in the dining room," Edith said. "Your table is just a little too small for a family meal. You may have to rethink that when you move out to the country." Edith offered a sly smile as she bustled down the hall and into her kitchen.

Beautifully modernized, it was a large room with plenty of space for the antique walnut table that sat against one wall, two mismatched chairs on either side of it. "You three get settled. I'll get the game."

"Would you like me to set the dining room table while

you do that?" Maggie asked, glad for any task that would get her out of the same room as Kane.

"Sure. You know where the plates are. Nothing fancy today since it's just pizza with friends, but do use the table-cloth. It always makes things seem festive. It's in the china cabinet. You boys can set up the game when I get back."

Boys?

Maggie glanced at Kane, barely hiding her amused smile.

He grinned, flashing straight white teeth.

Not a boy.

A man.

And that was a fact Maggie couldn't seem to ignore no matter how much she might want to.

She opened a cupboard and pulled out a handful of plates, her heart beating just a little too hard and fast. She opened another cupboard, pulled out a stack of plastic cups, then started to carry them across the room.

"Looks like you might need some help." Kane took the entire stack from her hands, his fingers brushing hers, the spicy scent of his aftershave drifting around them.

"Really, I'm fine. You and Eli should just stay here so you can set up the game—"

But Kane was already gone, out the door, probably in the dining room setting the table while Maggie stood in the kitchen trying to protest.

"Don't worry, Ms. Tennyson, I'll set up the game," Eli offered solemnly.

"Thanks, Eli."

By the time Maggie walked into the dining room, Kane had already set the cups and plates in a stack on the table.

"This table is big enough for an army," he commented, and Maggie nodded.

"Edith has a large family. You only saw about half of them the other night. If you can just lift the plates and cups for a minute, I'll look for the tablecloth."

"Lots of kids, huh?" He stepped aside while she rummaged through the china cabinet, found the tablecloth and spread it out on the table.

"Just three, but each of them gave her a truckload of grandkids. I think she was up to fifteen at last count. Plus three great-grandkids."

"Wow!"

"Yeah, things can get pretty loud here at Christmas. There. All set." She smoothed the tablecloth, then gestured for Kane to put the plates and cups down. "You can just put those anywhere, and I'll take care of the rest."

"In other words, you want me to leave."

"I just figured you'd want to go help Eli with the game."

"Really? Because I was thinking I make you uncomfortable."

"You don't." Much.

"Then why do you keep trying to avoid being in the same room as me?"

"What makes you think I'm doing that?"

"The fact that every time I enter a room, you leave it."

"I haven't done that."

"But you'd like to."

"Look, Kane." She turned from the plates she was setting out and faced him, her heart leaping as she looked into his emerald eyes.

"What?"

Good question. What *had* she planned to say?

"You're Eli's father, a man I barely know, and suddenly we're having pizza and playing games on Sunday afternoon. I'm not sure it's a good idea."

"Why not?"

"Because…just because." She turned back around, placed the last of the plates and set the cups down with a little more force than necessary. She expected Kane to leave. Was waiting for him to leave.

He didn't.

"I'm sure Edith has found the game. Shouldn't you go help set it up?"

"I will, but I want you to know something before I do." Kane's hands cupped her shoulders, and he urged her around to face him. "I didn't mean to barge into your life, but I have, and I'm not going to back out of it now."

"I don't expect you to. I know that Eli feels comfortable with me, and I know that he needs someone familiar in his life. I'm happy to give him that." She eased away from his touch, but the warmth of his hands lingered.

"I'm not just doing this for Eli. I think you know that."

"Dad! Ms. Edith sent me to get you. She says we need to get the game ready, and she said the pizza is probably burnt." Eli skidded into the room, cutting off further conversation.

"I'd better go check on it," Maggie said, nearly running from the room and from Kane, from whatever it was he might have said if his son hadn't interrupted.

I'm not just doing this for Eli.

Then who was he doing it for?

Himself?

Maggie?

Did she even want to know?

She shoved open the door to her apartment and considered slamming it closed and locking it, but Eli would be disappointed if she didn't bring down the pizza and play the game. Edith would be worried, and she'd come look-ing for Maggie.

Or worse, she'd send Kane.

Maggie hurried into the kitchen and took the pizza out of the oven. The cheese was bubbly and brown, the crust golden. It was perfect, and Maggie knew she couldn't put off the inevitable. She had to carry the pizza down into the dining room, sit with Kane and Eli and Edith and eat with them.

"It's not like it's a big deal," she said to herself as she made her way back through the apartment. The phone rang, but she ignored it. The sooner she got the afternoon over with, the better.

Edith was waiting for her as she walked into the dining room, her eyes shining with curiosity. "I sent the boys down to the basement to grab a few bottles of soda. I figured if you were providing the food, I could provide the drink."

"Thanks, I'll go get ice." Maggie set the pizza on the table and scooped up the cups.

"Hold on a minute, Maggie. You really think I don't have soda in the fridge? I sent them down so I could ask you something."

"What's that?"

"What in the world is going on?"

"I'm not sure I know what you're talking about."

"I'm talking about you and Eli and that good-looking father of his. Sitting at church together. Then playing games and having pizza together."

"Eli's having a tough time. I'm trying to help him ease into his new life."

"You expect me to believe that's all there is to it?"

"Yes, because that *is* all there is to it," Maggie hissed as the sound of Eli and Kane returning echoed down the hall.

"Smells good in here." Kane entered the room with a bottle of grape soda in his hand, and Edith frowned.

"Grape?"

"Eli thought we'd all enjoy it."

"In that case, it looks wonderful. Maggie is going to get ice, and then we'll pray and eat. And then..." She paused for dramatic effect. "I'm going to trounce every one of you at Monopoly."

"No way! *I'm* going to win," Eli said, laughing, and Maggie smiled as she went to get the ice.

At least someone was having a good day, and that was what the idea of lunch and ice cream had been about. Giving Eli a good time, helping him relax with his father, bringing the two of them a little closer.

"Edith told me you needed help carrying the glasses back." Kane's voice was so surprising, Maggie nearly dropped the cup she'd just filled with ice.

She whirled around, her pulse racing. "Edith is good at bossing people around."

"I'm learning that."

"Here you go." Maggie handed Kane two glasses.

"Thanks, and thanks for today. It's good to hear my son laugh again."

"You can thank Edith for that one."

"You brought the two of them together."

"Eli is a special kid, Kane, and I want to help him in any way I can."

"You're a good person."

"No. I'm not. I'm just someone doing the best I can." She offered a smile and headed back to the dining room, her pulse still racing.

Would Kane think she was a good person if he knew everything about the kind of life she'd lived in Miami? Would he think it if he knew that she'd worked as an exotic dancer at night and spent her days pursuing one thrill after another?

No. Maggie wasn't good.

She was simply forgiven.

"Are we ready to eat? I'm starved," Eli said as she set an ice-filled cup in front of him.

"We sure are," she replied, settling into a chair next to Edith.

"Shall we ask the Lord's blessing on the meal?" Edith held out her hands, and Maggie clasped one. Eli hesitated, then clasped the other.

And that's when Maggie realized that to complete the circle, she would have to hold Kane's hand.

She could be childish and refuse to take it, or she could act like the mature adult she sometimes was and do what needed to be done.

She placed her hand in his and felt warmth shoot up her arm, felt his fingers tighten fractionally.

"Kane, would you mind asking the blessing for us?"

"Not at all." He bowed his head, and Maggie did the same, her heart thumping too fast and too hard.

She should *not* be having this kind of reaction to Kane.

She should not be having *any* reaction to him.

As soon as the prayer was over, she tugged her hand away, grabbed the pizza cutter Edith had set on the table and began slicing the pie, studiously avoiding Kane's eyes while she did so.

She'd eat the pizza and play the game, but she would not let herself relax around Kane. She would not allow herself to think of him as a friend.

Or something more.

That was the plan, but as she set a slice of pizza on Kane's plate, caught his easy grin as he watched his son sipping grape soda, Maggie started to relax. Started to enjoy the easy conversation around the table.

By the time the meal was finished and the Monopoly game ended, she could barely remember what she'd been so worried about. Kane was charming, but he had paid no more attention to Maggie than he had to Edith. Obviously fatigue and fear had made her overreact to what she'd felt when Kane had held her hand. Obviously, it had made her overthink his words and his gestures. He was a nice guy, doing his best to create a loving home for his son. To think he'd have any time or energy left to devote to a relationship with a woman was ridiculous.

"How about that ice cream?" Edith asked as Eli carefully put away the game pieces.

"Maybe we could have pie, too," the nine-year-old responded hopefully.

"Eli, it's not polite to ask for food when you're at someone else's house." Kane pulled his cell phone from his pocket, glanced at it and frowned.

"Do you think they're finished running the tests on your sister?" Maggie asked.

"My parents would have called me if they were. At this point, I'm hoping that no news is good news."

"Is your sister ill?" Edith asked.

"I'm afraid so."

"I'm so sorry. I'll have my Bible study group pray for her. Can you write her name down for me? My memory just isn't what it should be."

"Sure." Kane accepted the paper and pen Edith held out, and scribbled his sister's name.

"Thank you. Now, about that pie. I've got so much left over, I'll be eating it for weeks. I'm more than happy to share it with my favorite young redhead. As for ice cream, all I have is vanilla, but I have plenty of that, too." She smiled at Eli, and he beamed back.

"I've got chocolate ice cream upstairs. Do you want any, Eli?"

"Eli? What about me? I'm a regular chocolate fanatic, Maggie, so you just go right on ahead and get it." Edith rose from the table and crossed the room.

Maggie followed, jogging up the stairs and into her apartment, more lighthearted than she'd been in days. Spending time laughing and enjoying herself was exactly what she'd needed.

The light on the answering machine was flashing as she walked into the living room, and she pushed Play as she passed it.

She'd grabbed the ice cream from the freezer and was walking out of the kitchen when the message began to play.

"Hey, babe. It's been a long time. Bet you thought you'd never hear from me again."

The voice froze her in her tracks and made the hair on the back of her neck stand on end.

"I saw you on TV. You're looking good. Better than ever. The car business is booming, but as soon as things slow down, I plan on coming for a little visit and taking up where we left off. Bet you're looking forward to that as much as I am."

The message cut off, but Maggie could still hear the voice. Derrick's voice, crawling along her nerves, making her muscles weak and her blood cold.

He'd found her.

She'd known it when Justin had tried to murder her, but until she'd heard Derrick's voice, she'd hoped she was wrong.

She hadn't been.

And now Derrick was coming to Deer Park. Coming to pick up where they'd left off, coming to finish what he'd begun the day he'd put his hands around her throat and tried to choke the life out of her.

She shuddered, the ice cream dropping from her hands as she ran to the phone and dialed the sheriff's office.

TWELVE

Kane stepped back into the kitchen, smiling as Eli looked up from a huge plate of apple pie and ice cream. Edith sat next to him, nursing a cup of coffee, a small piece of pie untouched on a plate nearby.

"Got enough pie and ice cream, sport?" Kane asked.

"Ms. Edith said I can take it home if I can't finish it all. She'll wrap it up for me and everything."

"In that case, dig in."

"Everything okay with your sister?" Edith stood, grabbed a plate from a cupboard and cut a slice of pie, handing it to Kane without bothering to ask if he wanted it.

"She's doing okay. They're still giving her fluids, but the test results were negative. No cancer."

"Wonderful! I know your whole family must be relieved."

"Yeah, after two years of chemo she's ready for a reprieve, and we're all hoping she'll get one."

He glanced around, frowning when he realized that Maggie wasn't in the dining room.

Where *was* she? Hadn't she come back yet?

Maybe the chocolate ice cream had been her excuse to escape. Although it had seemed like she'd been enjoying herself. She'd laughed and joked as she lost the Monopoly game, then cheered on Eli as he won.

"Is Maggie still upstairs?" he asked.

"Yes, and I can't figure out why. It takes all of two minutes to walk up those stairs and down again. I would have gone up to check on her, but I didn't want to leave Eli in here on his own."

"I appreciate that. I think I'll go up and make sure she's okay. Then Eli and I will get back to the hotel. We've taken up way too much of your afternoon."

"Hardly. Although I am playing at the evening service tonight, and that starts in an hour."

"I'll hurry." Kane jogged up the stairs, knocked on Maggie's door and frowned when it creaked open under his fist.

"Maggie?" He stepped into her small living room, frowning again when he saw a half gallon of ice cream lying on the floor.

"Maggie?" Adrenaline pumped through him as he stepped down the short corridor, peered in the kitchen, then the small bathroom.

There was one other door, and Kane knocked, his body tense with expectancy. Something had happened, and whatever it was hadn't been good. "Maggie, are you in there?"

"Yes." Her voice was muffled, and it sounded like she'd been crying.

"Can I come in?"

"No. I'm…not feeling well. Can you tell Eli that I'm sorry I missed out on the ice cream?"

"What's going on, Maggie?" He turned the doorknob, expecting it to be locked and feeling surprised when the door swung open to reveal the interior of the room.

Maggie sat cross-legged on a bed, her face devoid of

color, her eyes wide with surprise. "Don't you know you're not supposed to come into someone's room unless you're invited?"

"Technically, I'm not in your room. I'm at the threshold."

"And technically, I'm not angry. I'm just completely annoyed," she muttered, but there was little heat in her words.

"Sorry, but Edith was worried about you. So was I."

"Neither of you needed to be. I'm right here, sitting on my bed, safe as can be."

"You said you weren't feeling well."

She shrugged, getting up and walking past him out into the hall and to the living room. He followed, watching as she picked up the ice cream and put it in the freezer. Her movements were tight and tense, her muscles taut.

She didn't look ill. She looked exactly like what she'd said she was—annoyed.

"Something happened when you came up to the get the ice cream." He didn't phrase it as a question, knowing she wouldn't answer. "Did you hear from your ex?"

She tensed even more at his words, swinging around to face him. "I heard from him. He said he plans to pay me a visit and that we're going to pick up where we left off."

"Where was that?"

"What?" She brushed a loose strand of hair behind her ear and stared at him blankly.

"Where did the two of you leave off? Was he stalking you?"

"No."

"Abusing you?"

"I'd rather not talk about it."

"So he was." Just the thought made Kane's blood boil,

and he wanted to fly to Miami and knock some sense into the guy.

"I said I don't want to talk about it," she snapped, and seemed as surprised by her outburst as he was. "I'm sorry. It's not your fault." She took a deep breath and tried to smile.

"I know you don't want to talk about it, Maggie, but if you don't tell me what's going on, I can't help you."

"I don't want you to help me. I want you to take care of your son. Make sure he's okay. That's what's really important."

"You're important, too, and I'm not going to walk away from you. I'm not going to let you face your ex alone."

She frowned. "According to the sheriff, I won't be facing him at all."

"You called him?"

"Yes, and he said my ex is still in Miami, that leaving a message on my answering machine wasn't a crime and that as long as I wasn't overtly threatened there was nothing that could be done."

Kane's anger surged again. He'd have to have a chat with the sheriff, see exactly what it was that was keeping the man from acting on the information Maggie had provided.

"Did you erase the message?"

"No."

"Good. Can I hear it?"

She hesitated, and Kane took her hand, squeezed lightly. "You've given me my son back, Maggie. Let me do something for you. Let me help."

"There's nothing you can do to help, but if you want to hear it, I'll play it for you." She tugged her hand away, walked to the answering machine and pressed the button.

Kane stood beside her as the thug's voice filled the room. The guy was smart. He didn't say anything threatening. Didn't even hint that he might have something else on his agenda besides reconnecting with an old girlfriend.

But Kane had dealt with men like him before, had met enough of them during his days as a prosecuting attorney to know a con man when he heard one.

"You said his name was Derrick. What's his last name?"

"It doesn't matter."

"Sure it does. If I have his name, I can find the guy. If I can find him, I can stop him."

"From what? Like the sheriff said, he hasn't made any threats. Besides, you have enough to worry about without getting mixed up in my troubles."

"I'm already mixed up in them. Our lives connected the day you went to the sheriff and told him what you suspected about my son. I keep telling you that, and I keep meaning it."

"Kane—"

"Would you change what you did for me and Eli?"

"No. Of course not."

"And I wouldn't change the fact that you and I have met and that there's a connection between us."

"There's no…" Her voice trailed off and she shook her head.

"There is, Maggie. You can't deny it any more than I can."

"Maybe you're right. Maybe I can't." She took a deep breath and looked him straight in the eye, all her worry, all her fear obvious. "But admitting it doesn't change anything. I'm scared for Eli. I'm scared for you. I would never, ever forgive myself if something happened to either of you because of me."

"Then we've got a problem, because I'd never forgive myself if something happened to you because I turned my back and walked away when you needed me."

"I don't need you."

"You're wrong about that, Maggie. We need each other. Haven't you felt it when we're together? The way we click? The way it just seems to feel right when we're near each other?"

"Feelings don't mean anything." But her voice shook, and Kane knew she felt exactly what he did. Knew exactly what he was talking about.

"Sometimes they mean everything." He leaned down, did what he'd been wanting to all afternoon. Let his lips press against hers, let his hands settle on her waist.

She stiffened, then relaxed, her arms twining around his neck, pulling him closer.

And he went willingly, her fragrant perfume drifting around them, subtly intoxicating, wholly compelling. His hands swept up her back, tangled in her ponytail, tugging it loose from the band so that it fell around her shoulders in silky waves.

"Dad? Ms. Tennyson?" Eli's voice carried up the stairs, and Maggie jumped back, her cheeks flaming.

"Right here, sport," Kane called out, his voice husky, his heart pounding loudly in his ears as he watched Maggie sweep her hair up back into a ponytail.

"We shouldn't have done that," she said, her fingers touching her lips and then falling away.

"Maybe not, but I'm not going to say I'm sorry we did," Kane responded as Eli bounded into the apartment.

"What are you two doing?" Eli asked, his gaze jumping from Eli to Maggie and back again.

"Just talking," Maggie responded, offering Eli a quick smile.

"About dating? Because you look all red in the face like you're embarrassed, and I think talking about dating is probably embarrassing."

"Eli!" Kane and Maggie spoke together, and Kane laughed. Maggie didn't seem quite as amused. Although he thought he saw a hint of a smile at the corners of her mouth.

"What? Dating is a natural thing," Eli responded with a valiant attempt to appear older than his nine years.

"Who told you that?"

"Ms. Edith."

"You were discussing dating with Edith?" Maggie looked both horrified and fascinated, her pink cheeks and kiss-stained lips making Kane want to lean in and press his lips to hers once more.

"We were wondering what was taking you so long, and she said we were going to give you ten minutes and then I was going to come up to make sure you weren't getting into trouble."

"She didn't."

"I did," Edith called from just outside the door, and Maggie stalked across the room.

"I cannot believe you sent a nine-year-old to chaperone us."

"Did you need it?"

"Edith!"

"What? I'm a nosey old woman. I can't help myself."

"You're not old, Ms. Edith," Eli said. "You're beautiful, and you make the best apple pie in the whole world." Eli grabbed Edith's hand and patted it gently. Whatever Susannah had done wrong, she hadn't been cruel to Eli. The more time Kane spent with his son, the more he realized that. Cruelty, after all, begets cruelty, and despite his confusion and his sometimes sullen demeanor, Eli had a very tender heart.

"Are you trying to sweet talk me into sending more pie home with you, young man? Because if you are, it's working."

"Maybe you could bring it to the potluck, instead. Ms. Tennyson invited me and Dad, and we're going to come. Right, Dad?"

"Yes, but right now, we have to head home. Grandma and Grandpa will be back at the hotel soon, and we're going to pack up and get ready for tomorrow. You haven't forgotten that we're moving into our house, have you?"

"No. Goodbye, Ms. Edith. Goodbye, Ms. Tennyson. I had a lot of fun with you today." Eli offered a shy smile, and when Kane steered him toward the steps, he didn't pull away, didn't even tense beneath Kane's touch.

Spending time with Maggie and Edith had been good for him. It had been good for both of them. The stress of their reunion and the anxiety over Jenna's health had sapped some of the joy out of what should have been one of the best times of either of their lives.

They were back together again. A family again. Just the way Kane had dreamed they would be. And he wanted to enjoy every minute of it, cherish every second.

Outside, the sky was deep cerulean, the clouds pure white as the sun began its descent behind distant mountains. Kane took a deep breath, inhaling the fresh, clean scent of the air and for the first time in a long time he felt utter peace. Utter contentment.

Thank you, Lord, for a good afternoon. Thank you for the gift of my son. And for Maggie.

The kiss they'd shared had touched something deep in his soul, reminded him of what it meant to be truly connected to someone, and made him even more determined to find Maggie's ex-boyfriend.

Days ago he'd told her that she was family, but he hadn't realized then just how quickly she'd burrowed into his life, into his thoughts, even into his heart.

He glanced in the rearview mirror, saw that Eli had turned on a handheld game system, and pulled his phone out.

First he'd call the sheriff and see what he had to say. Then he'd call Skylar and get her searching for any Derrick who'd been in trouble with Miami PD in the past five years. Eventually, they'd track the guy down, and when they did, Kane planned to send a visitor to let Maggie's ex know just how foolish he'd be to keep coming after her. Hopefully, the guy would get the hint. He'd better because if anything happened to Maggie, Kane would hunt him down and make sure he spent the rest of his life paying for what he'd done.

He frowned.

Scratch that.

Nothing was going to happen to Maggie because Kane was going to find her ex before the scum had a chance to strike again. Maggie hadn't admitted she'd been abused, but she hadn't denied it, either. Her ex was a criminal, pure and simple, and Kane knew just how to deal with guys like him. Dig up the dirt, turn over every rock, uncover every crime from shoplifting to murder, and then prosecute to the fullest extent of the law.

It would happen.

Kane planned to make sure of it.

He smiled grimly as he lifted the phone and dialed the sheriff's office.

THIRTEEN

Maggie had been enjoying Wednesday night potluck at church for the better part of three years. It was something she looked forward to. A middle-of-the-week break from teaching and college. A time to fellowship with friends and neighbors. The fact that Eli and Kane were going to be there shouldn't have changed that, but somehow it did.

Kane had kissed her.

She'd kissed him back.

And she hadn't been able to stop thinking about it, no matter how hard she tried.

She ran a brush through her hair, her reflection in the bathroom mirror eliciting a sigh. There were deep circles beneath her eyes and fear had gauged hollows beneath her cheekbones. Derrick hadn't called again, but each time the phone rang she jumped, terror beating a hard, hollow rhythm in her chest.

That had been his point, of course. To leave her wondering when he'd call again, when he might show up behind her at the grocery store or outside the window at the school where she taught. To make her wonder if she'd find him in the backseat of her car, hunkered down and waiting for her to get behind the wheel. Or if she'd see him in her rearview mirror, staring at her from a car right behind her on the road.

Maggie shuddered, turning away from her reflection. The sheriff had assured her that Derrick was still in Miami and that the local police there were keeping an eye on him. He continued to believe that Justin had been working alone when he'd gone to Maggie's house and tried to kill her.

And Maggie wanted desperately to believe he was right.

But she couldn't.

The tentacles of Derrick's drug business were far reaching, and there was no doubt in Maggie's mind that he'd either hired Justin or found someone who would. Doing so would have been as easy for Derrick as creating a lesson plan was for Maggie.

Maybe eventually Justin would admit the truth, but until he did, the Miami police could take no action against Derrick, and Maggie would continue to jump at every shadow, wince at every creak and groan of the old house and freeze whenever the phone rang.

She set the brush down, grabbed her purse, her coat, and the Bundt cake she'd made for the potluck and hurried outside. It was getting late, the sun sinking low behind the mountains. Soon it would be dark, the shadows blending together, hiding anyone who might lurk nearby. She shivered, holding her coat closed as she hurried to her car. She fumbled in her purse, wishing she'd thought to have her keys in hand when she left the house. Wasn't that one of the rules of safety?

Not that having her keys in hand would save her from a bullet.

Maggie glanced around, a warning humming along her nerves as she finally managed to pull her keys out.

Was someone hiding in the shadows and watching her?

Was he going to attack as she got into the car? Force her to drive to some distant location where he'd—

She pulled her thoughts up short.

She wouldn't go there.

Wouldn't allow herself to dwell in the fear.

God was with her. Nothing that happened was outside of His control. She needed to remember that.

Her fists gripped the steering wheel as she drove to the church, all the tension from the past week tightening the muscles in her neck and shoulders. Her stitches itched and pulled and her head pounded, and she wanted to turn the car around and go back home.

She would have if Eli hadn't been expecting to see her at church.

But he was, and she couldn't disappoint him. Not after he'd told her at recess that afternoon that he and his father were making marshmallow crispy treats to bring and that he was going to wrap one especially for her.

He was such a sweet kid.

She'd miss him when he went to live in New York.

She'd miss his father, too, but that was another thing she refused to let herself dwell on.

Several people were walking from their cars to the church as Maggie pulled into the parking lot. She grabbed the cake and hurried to join them. There was safety in numbers, after all.

If Kane and Eli had already arrived, she didn't see them as she set the cake on the dessert table. Maybe Kane had changed his mind about bringing Eli. Maggie ignored the twinge of disappointment she felt at the thought. Keeping her distance was the best thing she could do for all of them, and she should be happy if the two didn't arrive.

Should be, but she had enjoyed Sunday afternoon, had even found herself imagining what it would be like to spend more time with Eli and Kane. As much as she wanted to deny it, Kane had been right when he'd said that they seemed to fit together. Not just Kane and Maggie, but the three of them. They were a team, working together to make something wonderful out of a difficult situation.

We need each other.

That's what Kane had said, and Maggie had wanted to deny it, but she couldn't.

"Ms. Tennyson, we're here! And Dad said we can sit with you if you want," Eli called out, and Maggie turned to face him. He looked adorable, his red hair mussed, freckles dotting his cheeks and nose. Kane was a few steps behind him, carrying the plate of promised marshmallow crispy treats.

He searched Maggie's face as he approached, and she wondered if he'd spent as much time thinking about her as she had about him. Her cheeks heated, but she refused to look away. "I'd love for you to sit with me, Eli. I was starting to worry that you weren't going to come."

"We would have been here sooner, but Grandma and Grandpa thought they might come. Then Aunt Jenna got sick again, and they decided to stay home."

"I'm sorry to hear that. Was the E.R. doctor able to give her any idea of what might be wrong?" She met Kane's eyes again, and her heart danced a happy jig.

"She has the flu. The doctor said it'll take a week or so before she's back to normal."

"Is there anything I can do for her?"

"She'd love to meet you, but I think that'll have to wait until after she's feeling better. I'm going to put this with the other food." He held up the plate. "If you and Eli want to find a seat, I'll join you in a minute."

"Where do you want to sit, Eli?" she asked, trying to still the wild beating of her heart.

"Anywhere. Oh, and before I forget, here." Eli reached into his coat pocket and pulled out a plastic-wrapped marshmallow crispy treat. "I asked my dad to cut one special just for you. See? It's a heart shape."

Maggie took the offering, smiling as she saw the carefully cut heart, her own heart doing a different kind of dance. A softer one. "It's wonderful."

"Are you going to eat it?"

"It's too special to eat," she responded, wishing she could keep it forever. Despite the difficult circumstances they'd both found themselves in, she and Eli had formed a bond. Or maybe not *despite* the circumstances, maybe *because* of them.

"But it'll go bad if you don't eat it."

"Not if I put it in the freezer."

"The freezer?" Eli didn't sound convinced, and Maggie smiled, ruffling his hair.

"Sure. Then whenever I'm feeling down, I can take it out and look at it and remember that someone cared enough to give it to me." She pulled out a chair at one of the long tables and gestured for Eli to take a seat.

"Here, put my purse on the seat next to you, Eli, to save it for your father."

"Okay, but he might want to sit next to you, too."

"Why would you think that?"

"Because you're a woman and he's a man, and that's the kind of thing men and women do."

"You haven't been talking to Edith again, have you?"

"Nope. I was talking to Grandpa while we played chess. He was explaining things to me."

"What things?"

"Things like why your face gets all red when Dad smiles at you."

"My face does not get red when your father smiles at me." But it did, and Maggie knew it.

"Yes it does, but don't worry, you still look pretty. Not like Madeline Dillon. When her face gets red she looks like a lobster."

"I hope you didn't say that to her."

"I was going to, but Grandpa explained to me that girls don't like to hear stuff like that."

"It sounds like you're spending a lot of time playing chess with your grandfather."

"I have to if I'm ever going to get good enough to beat him. Where'd Dad go?"

"He went to put the marshmallow treats down, remember?"

"Yes, but he was over at that table across the room, and now he's gone. I don't see him anywhere."

Neither did Maggie.

She stood, searching the crowded room, trying to spot Kane, but he was nowhere to be found. "You're right. I don't see him."

"Do you think he went home and left me?" Eli sounded panicky, his eyes wide with fear.

"Of course he didn't. Maybe he left something in the car and had to go get it."

"Like what?"

"His cell phone? He's been worried about your aunt. He wouldn't want her to be unable to reach him if she needed to."

"He always carries his cell phone in his pocket."

"Then maybe he left his wallet or…" What? Maggie couldn't think of anything that made sense. But, then, it didn't make sense that Kane was gone. No way would he walk away and leave his son.

She scanned the room again, doing a three-sixty but still not spotting Kane.

"He's probably mad at me. He probably doesn't want to be my father anymore." Eli's voice broke, and Maggie sat down again, put an arm around his shoulder and pulled him close.

"Of course he's not angry with you. Even if he was, he'd still want to be your father."

"But I'm difficult. My moth—Susannah said so. She said I was lucky to have her because no one else would want me."

"She was a very confused lady, Eli, and that had nothing to do with you. Whatever she said to you, it wasn't the truth." Maggie glanced around the room again, more worried than she wanted to admit. Where *was* Kane?

She was about to stand up again, to take Eli around and ask if anyone had seen Kane leave, when she saw him walk back into the room carrying a large slow cooker. "There he is, Eli. It looks like he was helping someone carry in some food."

Eli looked in the direction Maggie was pointing and the anxiety eased from his face. "Oh. Okay."

"I told you he wouldn't leave you."

Eli just nodded, picking at the plastic tablecloth and avoiding Maggie's gaze. He was embarrassed, and Maggie knew he was ready to drop the subject. She'd have to tell Kane what had happened, but not now. Not with Eli nearby.

"Sorry I took so long," Kane said as he took the seat beside his son. "One of the ladies asked for help bringing something in."

"It looks like you made it just in time. The pastor is getting ready to pray."

"Good. I'm starved. How about you, sport?" Kane asked, and Eli shrugged. Apparently, he wasn't willing to forget the anxiety his father had caused.

The tension between father and son was obvious as the pastor asked the congregation to join him in prayer. He asked a blessing on the food and the gathering and then invited everyone to dig in.

"You guys ready to get some food?" Maggie knew her tone was too cheerful and bright, but neither Kane nor Eli seemed to notice. They both got up and walked to the food line with her, and the tension seemed to dissipate as the cheerful good humor of the rest of the crowd washed over them.

"Hey, Eli! Wait up!" A dark-haired boy ran to join them, his deeply tanned face set in a happy smile. Seth Whitmore was another student in the fourth-grade class where Maggie taught. Bright and vivacious, he was friends with everyone and had made an extra effort to include Eli in his circle of buddies.

"Hi, Seth."

"I didn't know you went to church here."

"My dad and I just started coming."

"Cool. Want to sit with me and the other guys? We're over there." He gestured to a table not far from where Maggie, Eli and Kane had been sitting.

Eli looked at his father, who gave a subtle nod.

"Okay, I guess."

"Great. Hey, guess what? My mom made hot wings to bring. You like hot wings, right?"

"Yes."

"Well, these are the best ever. Take a lot of them because we brought plenty."

The two boys continued to exchange opinions about food as they grabbed plates and piled them high. Maggie grabbed a plate, too, and had just scooped up some pasta salad when she realized that she and Kane were going to go back to the table and sit together *without Eli.*

That was definitely *not* how she had planned the evening to go. She frowned, stabbing a piece of fried chicken with a serving fork and shaking it onto her plate.

"Looks like that you've got a bone to pick with that chicken," Kane said wryly.

"I think I've got a bone to pick with just about everyone tonight." She kept her response light, her attention focused on the table of food.

"Rough day?"

"Rough week."

"I have some news that might make it better," he said, pulling out her chair before he took a seat in the one Eli had vacated.

"What's that?"

"I've found some interesting information about your ex."

"My ex?"

"Derrick Lyons. Used-car salesman to some. Drug supplier to many."

At his words, Maggie froze, dropping the piece of chicken she'd been about to bite into. "How did you find that out?"

"The sheriff and I had a talk after I left your place on Sunday night."

"And he told you Derrick's name?"

"No. He told me that he had things under control. I wasn't too happy to get the brush-off, so I decided to do some research and see what I could find out."

"So you invaded my privacy?" Maggie hissed, her stomach twisting with anger and dismay. He had no right to investigate her past, but he had done so anyway, and now he knew it all. The life she'd led. The mistakes she'd made. The person she'd once been.

"I would never do that."

"What do you mean, you'd never do it? You did." Maggie picked up her plate, walked blindly across the room and dumped it into a trash can.

She was halfway to the door when Kane put a hand on her arm, holding her in place. "I found your ex to protect you, Maggie. Your past is your business."

"It was my business. Now it's yours. Next it will be everybody's."

"You know that's not true."

She did.

Of course, she did.

Kane wasn't the kind of person to spread information that was meant to be private.

But that wasn't the point.

The point was, he'd dug into her past. He'd found out everything there was to know about her life before Deer Park, and just thinking about it made her cheeks flame.

She pulled away, took a step toward the door. "I need to go home."

"You don't need to run away, Maggie. Nothing has changed between us."

"Everything has changed," she whispered, glancing around hoping they weren't attracting attention. Humiliation piled on humiliation was the last thing she needed.

"You'd already told me part of your past. Eventually, you would have told me everything." His words were soothing; his eyes so filled with compassion, Maggie could barely look in them.

"Maybe I would have. *Probably* I would have, but you didn't give me that option. And now…"

"What?"

"I've spent three years being Maggie Tennyson. Wholesome girl-next-door. Teacher-in-training. Church member. And suddenly I'm Angel Simmons again. The kid with big dreams of making a better life for herself. The one who only managed to make a mess of things."

"Maggie—" He reached for her hand, and she could see the regret in his eyes. He hadn't meant to hurt her.

But she was hurt.

Maybe not by him as much as by her own failures, by the truth of her life laid bare for others to see.

"I need to go. Tell Eli I'm sorry I ran out on him again. I'll see him at school tomorrow," she managed. And then she turned and ran. From Kane's compassionate gaze. From the easy laughter and conversation of her church family. From her past and all that she wished she could change but couldn't.

Out to the car. Into it.

She turned the ignition and pulled onto the road, her throat tight with tears she refused to shed.

The road was empty and dark, and she thought she could drive for hours, days, even weeks and never escape what she was running from.

Herself. The person she'd been and that she'd promised herself she'd never again be.

Headlights appeared behind her, pulling out of the church parking lot and onto the road. Coming fast.

Kane?

No, he wouldn't have been able to get Eli and get into his car so quickly.

The headlights drew closer, and Maggie stepped on the

accelerator, unconsciously trying to put space between herself and whoever was coming.

But the car behind her sped up too, pulling so close it was nearly bumper-to-bumper with her Ford. She glanced in the rearview mirror and saw that the interior light was on in the other vehicle. Saw dark hair. A tan, swarthy face.

Her heart stopped and started again, her foot pressing down even harder on the accelerator. Her car jolted forward, Maggie's palms slipping as she tried to steer around a steep curve in the road. The Ford fishtailed, and Maggie's grip tightened.

Please, God, don't let it be him. Don't let it be.

The car pulled out from behind Maggie and pulled up beside the Ford, and Maggie looked. She had no choice. Had to know. And saw him grinning from the other car, his eyes deep, black sockets in a skeletal face.

It was every nightmare she'd ever had, every fear she'd ever experienced.

She screamed, jerking the Ford to the side, hearing metal grind against metal as she hit a guard rail.

The steering wheel nearly jerked from her hands, and she tightened her grip, managing to right the car before she completely lost control.

Derrick's car sped ahead, swerved in front of her and kept going, flying into the darkness, disappearing around a curve in the road.

Gone as quickly as it had appeared.

But not gone for long.

Maggie was as sure of that as she was of anything.

Her hands shook as she pulled out her cell phone and called 911. The operator told her to pull over and wait for help to arrive, and Maggie did, easing into the breakdown lane, her eyes straining to see into the darkness. Was Derrick out there somewhere, creeping toward her car? Was he easing through the pine trees that lined the road? Would he kill her before help arrived?

Should Maggie drive away? Should she stay?

She didn't know, couldn't decide.

So she waited, staring at the dashboard clock, counting the minutes and the wild thump of her heart until a police car pulled up behind her and an officer got out.

FOURTEEN

Kane rubbed the back of his neck and stared at the information lying on the desk in front of him in their new rental home. He'd been up half the night digging for more dirt about Maggie's ex. The three pages he'd printed out were mostly as bland as vanilla ice cream, but there were a few interesting morsels tossed in. He forwarded the data to Skylar with instructions to call Miami PD.

He had other things to do. Like figuring out how to apologize to Maggie. He'd been so bent on his mission to find Derrick that he'd done exactly what she'd accused him of—invaded her privacy. Just thinking about the words and the look on her face when she'd said them made him cringe. He hadn't meant to bring up a past that Maggie had worked hard to put behind her.

But he had.

And now he had to make things right.

He glanced down at the folder that contained everything he'd learned about Maggie. She'd grown up tough, and the wild life she'd lived during her teens and early twenties had been a reflection of that. An exotic dancer who'd worked at a popular club, Angel Simmons, whose driver's license photo a Miami police officer had accessed, barely resembled the woman Kane had come to care about. Still, he thought that if he'd met her three years ago, he would have recognized the qualities that attracted him now. Compassion, empathy, a tender spirit.

He lifted the folder, opened it to the photo and looked at it one last time. Angel Simmons. Maggie Tennyson. Lost soul. Now found. Her past was hers to keep, and he'd tell her that if she ever spoke to him again.

He shoved the folder through the shredder, let all the details of Maggie's past be eaten up.

"Kane? I'm sorry to interrupt, but Eli's principal is on the phone." Kane's mother appeared in the doorway, the phone in her hand, her palm covering the mouthpiece.

The principal?

That couldn't be good. Kane had walked Eli to school less than an hour ago. Had something happened since then?

He took the phone, his stomach knotted with concern. "Kane Dougherty speaking."

"Mr. Dougherty, it's Krista Mallory. I'm the principal at Deer Park Elementary. We spoke a few days after you got to town."

"I remember, Ms. Mallory. What can I do for you?" Kane raked a hand through his hair and paced across the room.

"I don't want to worry you, but Eli seems to be having… some issues."

"Issues? What kind of issues?" Kane tensed, not liking the word *issues* and feeling pretty sure it couldn't be mean anything good.

"He's in with the school nurse, complaining of a stomachache."

"My sister has been sick with the flu. He probably has the same. I'll be right there to pick him up." A stomachache

Kane could understand, the flu he could deal with. Both were better than "issues."

"The thing is, Mr. Dougherty, the nurse doesn't think he's sick."

"No?"

"Eli's teacher said he was fine when he arrived in class this morning. As a matter of fact, he was more outgoing and happy than he's ever been. Then he realized that the teacher's aide for the class wasn't going to be in…"

"Ms. Tennyson?"

"That's right. Eli found out she wouldn't be there, and he said he wanted to go home."

"I see."

"Of course, we couldn't allow that."

"And that's when he decided he had a stomachache?"

"I'm afraid so."

"I'll be there in a few minutes."

"I appreciate it, Mr. Dougherty, and I hope you understand that we wouldn't normally call a parent about something like this. But Eli is a special case, and we want to do whatever we can to help the transition into his new life go smoothly."

"I'd rather be called than not, so you made a good decision. Thanks." Kane hung up.

His mother and sister were hovering in the doorway. "Is everything okay?" his mother asked, and Kane nodded.

"The teacher's aide Eli is so fond of didn't show up at school today, and he's not taking it well."

"Maggie, you mean? Is she okay? I know you said she's been having some trouble with her ex." Jenna frowned, her words reflecting Kane's own concern.

"I don't know. I'm going to pick Eli up at school, and then I'm going to give her a call. Make sure she's all right."

"Well, if you need to go over and help her, you just go ahead and do it. Your father, sister and I can take care of Eli for the day. As a matter of fact, I think we'll bake some chocolate chip cookies. There's nothing like cookies hot out of the oven to cure what ails a child." Kane's mother bustled away, and Jenna smiled.

"Mom always did know how to make us feel better when we were kids," Jenna said.

"Yeah. I wish I were half as good with Eli."

"You will be, Kane. Once you get to know him."

"Maybe." Kane pulled on his coat and stepped outside. The day was gray, the sky heavy with clouds. The meteorologist was calling for snow, and Kane was sure he could smell it in the air.

The school was just two blocks away from the new house, but he decided to drive. The quicker he got to the school, the quicker he could find out what was going on with his son.

He pulled into the school parking lot, hurried inside and veered left into the office. An office assistant looked up as he entered and offered a smile.

"Mr. Dougherty, Principal Mallory said you were on your way. You can go right in to her office." She gestured to the door behind her desk, and Kane skirted the desk and a wall of file cabinets and stepped into the room.

An older woman with graying hair and a bright smile stood as he entered the room. "Hello, Mr. Dougherty. I'm Principal Mallory."

"Nice to meet you." Though he would have preferred doing so under other circumstances.

"Why don't you have a seat? My assistant is going to call down to the nurse's office, and Eli should be here shortly."

"Thanks." Kane perched on the edge of the chair, feeling

uncomfortable but not sure why. Generally, he was good in new situations and could handle whatever came his way with ease. But everything to do with Eli seemed a potential land mine, and he constantly had to remind himself to tread cautiously.

"While we have a minute, I'd like to thank you for making the decision to let Eli stay in school during this transitional time. It's good for him to have a sense of continuity in his life."

"I agree," Kane responded, wishing the nurse would hurry up with Eli. It wasn't that he didn't appreciate the principal's words of thanks, but he didn't feel like he deserved them. He hadn't done anything that any other parent wouldn't have done in the same circumstances.

"We've all been talking about it here at Deer Park Elementary, and we realize what a sacrifice it must be for you to leave a home in New York to settle in a small town like ours."

"It isn't a sacrifice to do something that benefits my son."

"I suppose not, but we want to make sure you know we're here to offer support in any way we can."

"I appreciate that, Principal Mallory, and I'll be sure to let you know if there's anything Eli needs." He'd heard similar words so often since he'd come to Deer Park that they'd almost become meaningless. Although he knew people meant well, there really wasn't anything any of them could do to help Eli through the very painful process of letting go of a woman he'd called mother for five years. Nor could anyone help him learn to embrace a man who'd been nothing more than a vague memory for most of Eli's life.

"Good. I think that's especially important since Ms. Tennyson won't be coming back for several weeks."

"Several weeks?" The conversation had suddenly become much more interesting, and Kane leaned forward, wanting to ask why Maggie would take several weeks off but feeling certain the principal wouldn't answer. It was Maggie's private business, after all.

And it was business Kane planned to stick his nose into once he figured out what was going on with his son.

"Yes. She'll be off through the month of December and plans to return after Christmas break."

"Eli will miss having her in the classroom."

"All of the children will, but she'll return as a full-time teacher after her graduation."

"Graduation?"

"She's been pursuing a degree in elementary education since she began working here. We're looking forward to officially giving her the title of teacher. She earned it long ago."

"She seems to have a way with kids."

"She does."

The sound of voices interrupted the conversation, and the principal stood. "It sounds like Eli has arrived. Thank you again for being such a good father to him."

Kane would have responded, but Eli appeared in the doorway, his hair mussed and his cheeks pale. "I'm sorry, Dad."

"For what?" Kane stood and put a gentle hand on his son's shoulder.

"For making you come get me."

"Nobody made me do anything. I wanted to come. Anytime you need me, I'll be here."

"My stomach was hurting."

"Does it feel better now?"

"I think so."

"Do you think you want to go back to class?"

"I'm not sure."

"I heard Ms. Tennyson isn't here today."

"And she's not going to be here until after Christmas, either." Eli blinked rapidly, and Kane was sure he was trying not to cry.

"She needs a few weeks off to study for her final exams," Principal Mallory cut in. "Do you know what they are?"

"No."

"They're very important tests that every college student must take before finishing a class."

"Ms. Tennyson is a teacher, not a student."

"She's a teacher's aide, and she can't officially be a teacher until she graduates from college."

"Oh."

"But don't worry, she'll be back after her finals, and when she does graduate, we'll make her an official teacher right here at Deer Park Elementary. Doesn't that sound wonderful?"

"I guess," Eli responded, staring down at the carpet rather than looking at the principal. Kane was tempted to correct the behavior but knew that would only embarrass Eli.

"I know you'll miss her, Eli, but I'm sure she'll come back to visit when she has time," Principal Mallory said gently.

Eli didn't look convinced, and Kane doubted there was anything more that could be said that would make a difference. Better to go home and let Grandma try her chocolate-chip-cookie cure on him.

"Are you ready to go home, Eli? Grandma is baking chocolate chip cookies, and I know she'd love for you to help."

Eli shrugged, and Kane decided to take that as a yes.

"Let's go then. Thank you again, Principal Mallory."

"You're quite welcome. We'll see you tomorrow, Eli." Principal Mallory offered Eli a bright smile and quick wave, and Eli nodded.

Kane took his son's hand and was surprised when he didn't pull away. Maybe they really were making progress.

Or maybe Eli was just too tired to continue fighting the tide that was dragging him into his new family.

"Is Grandma really making chocolate chip cookies?" Eli asked as he climbed into the SUV.

"I wouldn't have said it if it weren't true. Knowing Grandma, she's got all the ingredients out and the oven preheated, and she's waiting at the door for you to come home so she can get started."

"She and Grandpa are leaving on Friday."

"Yep."

"And Ms. Tennyson is gone. Is Aunt Jenna going to leave, too?" There seemed to be another question lurking beneath the one Eli voiced. Maybe "Are you going to leave?" Or "Do adults always go away?"

"Aunt Jenna is going to stay here for as long as we're here, and Ms. Tennyson hasn't gone anywhere. She's just taking a break from work so she can study."

"How do you know? Did you talk to her?"

"No, but Principal Mallory told us that's what she was doing."

"That doesn't mean it's true. People lie all the time."

Kane wasn't sure how to respond to that.

On the one hand, it was true. On the other hand, no nine-year-old should be as cynical as Eli.

He pulled into the driveway of the two-story brick colonial he'd rented and shifted to look at his son. "People do lie, Eli, but not all the time and not about something like what Principal Mallory told you."

Eli gave his trademark shrug and got out of the SUV.

Short of calling him back and trying to convince him of something he obviously wasn't going to believe, there wasn't much Kane could do but follow Eli to the house.

The front door flew open before they made it there, and Kane's mother stepped outside, a pink cardigan around her shoulders and a broad smile on her face. "There he is! Just the young man I wanted to see. You know what I need, Eli?"

"What?"

"An assistant chef, and you look like you'll fit the bill just right."

"Really? Dad said you were baking cookies."

"Not just cookies. My famous double-chocolate chocolate chip cookies. Grandpa and Aunt Jenna are out getting everything we need, and while they're gone we're going to have hot chocolate and play video games."

"You play video games?"

"Not yet, but for you, I'll learn. Come on." She turned and walked back into the house, and Eli followed willingly. Perhaps he was as fascinated with the idea of his grandmother playing video games as Kane was.

Kane stepped into the foyer but didn't bother taking off his coat. He didn't plan to stay long. "If you two will be okay together, I'm going to run a few errands."

His mother stopped halfway down the hall and turned to face Kane. "Are you going to call—"

"I'll stop by her place." He cut her off, not wanting Eli to know that he planned to contact Maggie.

His mother glanced at Eli, who was listening intently. "All right. How long will you be?"

"I should be home in a couple of hours. If anything comes up, I'll give you a call."

"Maybe I should come with you," Eli said, walking

toward Kane, and for the first time since they'd been reunited, Kane had the sense that his son really cared that they were together again.

"Then you'll miss out on baking those cookies."

"I don't mind."

"But Grandma might be disappointed. Besides, I won't be gone that long."

Eli hesitated, then nodded. "Okay. I'll see you when you get back, right?"

"Of course," Kane said, and he gave in to temptation and dropped a kiss on Eli's head. "See you guys in a little while."

He walked back outside before he could change his mind and invite Eli to come along. He needed to talk to Maggie, find out what had made her decide to take a month off of work, because he didn't believe the story she'd told Principal Mallory.

He pulled up in front of Edith's house and was surprised to see the sheriff's car parked in the driveway. Something *had* happened, and Kane was going to find out what.

He jogged up the porch stairs, knocked on the door and waited impatiently for Edith to open it.

She peered out a side window first, then cracked the door open. "Oh, good, it really is you."

"Did you think it would be someone else?"

"Him. Maggie's ex. You've heard about him, haven't you? How he tried to kill her in Miami? He's here. Somewhere in Deer Park, and the police can't find him," she whispered, stepping aside to let Kane inside.

"Is Maggie in her apartment?"

"Yes. Sheriff O'Malley has been up there with her for an hour. Didn't look happy when he got here. You'll probably want to wait until he comes down. Want a cup of coffee?"

"No, thanks. I think I'll go see what's happening."

"I don't know if the sheriff is going to like that."

"Good thing I'm not too concerned about what he thinks." Kane offered a brief smile and walked up the stairs.

He knocked twice before Maggie opened the door.

"Kane. What are you doing here?" Her eyes were deeply shadowed, her face devoid of color.

"I heard you were planning to take a few weeks off from work. I thought I'd come over to find out why."

"I'm a little busy right now. Maybe you can give me a call later," she said, glancing over her shoulder at the sheriff, who stood a few feet away.

"I don't mind waiting." He stepped into her apartment and nodded at the sheriff. "I left a couple of messages at your office, Sheriff O'Malley, but from what I hear, you've had plenty of other things to deal with."

"Unfortunately, that's true. Maggie ran into some trouble last night, and I've been concentrating my efforts on that."

"What kind of trouble?" Kane asked, turning his attention to Maggie.

"I saw Derrick last night. He was waiting in the church parking lot and pulled out after I left. He followed me for a couple of miles and then disappeared."

"You're sure it was him?"

"That's what Sheriff O'Malley keeps asking, and I keep telling him that I am. Derrick is in Deer Park. He pulled up behind my car with his interior lights on last night. I saw his face clearly."

"It can be difficult to see when headlights are shining into your eyes, Maggie. It's very possible the person you saw simply resembled your ex," the sheriff said wearily, as if he'd said the same a half dozen times.

"You said yourself that the Miami police haven't seen Derrick in two days. Why is it so hard to believe he could be here?" Maggie responded, her tone sharp.

"His friends and employees said he's on a fishing expedition."

"That doesn't mean that's actually where he is," Kane cut in, and the sheriff frowned.

"We're not discounting any possibilities. Miami PD is actively searching for Lyons on their end, and we're doing the same here."

"Then why do you keep asking me if I'm sure I saw him?" Maggie didn't try to hide her exasperation.

"When we bring him in, we're going to need evidence to hold him. I don't want to risk having the guy out on the street because we have no proof that he's threatening you."

It made sense from a legal perspective, but Kane doubted Maggie cared much about that. What she wanted to hear was that the police were going to find Derrick and put him in jail for good.

"The Miami PD should have plenty of that. I've had some people doing some digging and they've come up with information the police are going to find interesting."

"Yeah? What's that?" Sheriff Mallory took out a notebook and a pen and scribbled something on what looked to be an already filled page.

"A girlfriend of his left Miami a year ago. She died a few months later in a hit-and-run accident."

"People die in hit-and-run accidents every day." The sheriff wasn't convinced, and Kane knew what he was thinking. Coincidences happened. Circumstantial evidence wasn't enough to get a conviction. It's what Kane had been thinking until he'd dug deeper.

"I agree, but five years ago, the guy lost another girlfriend in a fluke fall from a balcony apartment. They'd both been drinking, and he said she climbed onto the balcony wall and fell."

"That happened in Miami, too?"

"San Antonio. He mentioned it to me once right after we met. He said it was the reason he moved to Miami. He wanted to escape the memories," Maggie cut in, flashing Kane a look that told him exactly what she thought of all the digging he'd been doing.

"Interesting, but bad things do happen, and I know plenty of people who have lost more than one family member in tragic accidents."

"Yeah? Well Lyons seems to have had a whole lot of bad luck when it comes to girlfriends. His high school girlfriend died of an overdose when she was five months pregnant with his child."

"He never wanted kids." Maggie spoke so quietly, Kane almost didn't hear her.

"What?"

"Derrick didn't want kids. He told me that over and over again—No kids. No way. No how. But he never mentioned his high school girlfriend. Never mentioned the baby they were going to have together." Maggie's voice trembled, and she swayed.

"You need to sit down." Kane took her arm.

"I'm okay."

"Maggie—"

"I am." But she took a seat anyway, settling onto the couch, her skin paper white.

"Maybe we should continue this outside." Sheriff O'Malley walked toward the door, but Maggie shook her head.

"This is more my business than anyone else's. I'd rather you stay."

Sheriff O'Malley hesitated, then nodded. "All right. What else have you got, Kane?"

"Just that the girlfriend died in San Francisco, California. Her friends said her death was suspicious. She was a cheerleader, an honor roll student. By all accounts a good kid who'd never touched drugs."

"And the police report?" the sheriff asked.

"No physical evidence to indicate anything but a tragic accidental overdose."

"Anything else?"

"That's it, but I think it's enough. Three women dead, and Maggie scared for her life. The guy is a killer, and he needs to be put away."

"You informed Miami PD of this?"

"I had an associate send an e-mail file. I was hoping you could give them a call and follow up on the information."

"No problem. Unfortunately, the information won't help us find Lyons. We've issued an APB on the guy, but there are a lot of back roads in Deer Park, plenty of places for a guy to hide if he wants to." The sheriff walked to the door and turned his attention to Maggie. "I'm going to run patrols down your street every hour, but if anything suspicious happens, call 911. We can have someone here in minutes."

"Thank you, Sheriff."

"We'll do everything we can to make sure Lyons doesn't get to you, and if he's in town, we'll find him." The sheriff walked out of the apartment and down the stairs.

Maggie stood with her hand on the open door, as if she were waiting for Kane to follow the sheriff out.

He ignored her subtle hint and walked toward her instead. "Are you okay?"

"I don't know." She closed the door, leaned against it,

her hand trembling as she brushed a lock of hair from her cheek. "I knew Derrick could be mean, but…"

"But what?" He took her hand, tugged her into his arms. She didn't resist. Just burrowed close, her head resting against his chest, her hair soft against his chin.

"Those three women. That unborn baby. How could anyone do such a thing?" Her voice broke, and Kane smoothed a hand down her back, wishing he had words of comfort to offer, some wisdom that would make a difference.

"I don't know."

"And how could I not have known what he was capable of?"

"How could you have? He's probably a sociopath. No conscience but plenty of charm."

"Still. I should have known. I probably *would* have known if I hadn't been so lost in my addiction. I told you before that I wasn't a good person, Kane. I wasn't lying." She took a deep, shuddering breath and stepped away, looking into his eyes, letting him see the sadness and shame she carried.

"You're wrong. You're a wonderful person, Maggie. Everything I know about you tells me that."

"Everything? Do you mean the fact that I was an exotic dancer or the fact that I would have sold my soul for my next hit?" She turned away, her back stiff, her words tight.

"Do you really think those things make a difference to me?"

"They should. You've got a son to worry about. The last thing he needs is someone like me in his life."

"Someone who cares, you mean? Someone who knows what it's like to struggle, who has been to hell and back, and can say 'I understand' and really mean it? I think that's the *first* thing he needs in his life."

She stiffened, but didn't respond.

"Maggie." He put a hand on her shoulder, urged her around, his heart shattering as he saw the tears on her cheeks. "I never meant to make you cry."

"You didn't."

"No?" He brushed away the moisture, watched as more tears fell.

"I had so many dreams when I was a kid. If I'd followed them, I could have been a different person."

"You *are* a different person."

"But my past is still part of who I am, Kane. Don't you see that? The person you thought I was, she doesn't exist."

"How could she not exist? She's standing right in front of me."

"You don't understand."

"I understand that your past made you who you are. I understand that who you are is exactly who I need in my life."

"Kane—"

"Have a little faith in that, Maggie." And he leaned down capturing her lips with his, sealing his words with a gentle promise.

"Knock, knock. It's your landlady." Edith opened the door and peeked inside. "Oops. Hope I'm not interrupting anything."

"You're not." Maggie's cheeks were bright pink as she stepped away from Kane and scrubbed the remnants of tears from her eyes.

"Too bad."

"Edith!"

"Well, you're both young and single, and you both love that little boy. What's the harm in hoping God might have big plans for you?"

"Speaking of little boys," Maggie said quickly, "how has Eli been doing? Since I wasn't at school today, we didn't get a chance to chat about how things are going."

"Actually, he's the reason why I'm here. He was upset when he found out you weren't coming to school for a few weeks. Principal Mallory had to call me to come get him."

"I'm so sorry. I should have thought of that."

"I think you had plenty to think about without worrying about Eli."

"I *am* worried about him, though."

"He's fine. My mother is making cookies with him, and I believe they were going to play video games together."

"That sounds like fun."

"It's just normal family stuff, but I think Eli is going to enjoy it."

"I remember when I was his age, I wanted nothing more than 'normal' family stuff."

"Well, there's absolutely no good reason why you can't have some normal family stuff now," Edith said, and Maggie frowned.

"What do you mean, Edith?"

"The obvious. Kane should invite you over to his place to bake cookies and play video games."

"That's a great idea, Edith." Kane smiled at the older woman, and she winked.

"No, it's not. Kane and his family need time alone to bond with Eli."

"Why that's just about the silliest thing I've ever heard. That boy needs his family, but he needs you, too. You're his stability, his anchor. You're not going to deny him that, are you?" Edith grabbed Maggie's coat from the closet as she spoke, then tossed it around Maggie's shoulders.

"But what about you? I can't leave you here with Derrick

on the loose. What if he comes looking for me and finds you, instead?"

"You think I'm afraid of that scoundrel? I'm not. Besides, there's an unmarked police car parked right across the street. The deputy came over a few minutes ago and introduced himself. See?" She gestured to a dark sedan parked across the street.

"Are you sure he's really a deputy?" Kane frowned, wondering if Edith had bothered asking for identification.

"Do you think I'm daft, young man? Of course I'm sure. He showed me his badge, and I called the sheriff to confirm it. He'll be here until dark, and then someone else will take his place."

"The sheriff said he was going to run patrols. He didn't say anything about an around-the-clock guard." Maggie glanced at the unmarked car, tensing as a man wearing a deputy uniform got out.

"That was before a few of his men volunteered for extra duty. We protect our own around these parts, don't we, Deputy Peterson?" Edith called out as the deputy approached.

"That's right. We'll do everything we can to keep you safe, Ms. Tennyson."

"I appreciate it."

"And so do I," Edith added. "Now, off you two go. I've got some friends coming over in an hour, and I've got a house to clean before then. Be good, and be home before dark."

Maggie laughed, but Kane could hear the tension in it. "You're incorrigible, Edith."

"I try. Now skedaddle."

"I'll take my own car," Maggie said, hurrying to her Ford and barely sparing Kane a glance. She was nervous or scared or both. Kane didn't blame her. Derrick was out there somewhere, and until he was found, she wouldn't be safe.

He glanced around as he got into his SUV. The day was bright and sunny, the sky clear. Kane wanted to believe the beauty of it was a harbinger of good things to come, but the sun had been shining the day his wife had died of a coronary embolism. The sky had been clear and beautiful the day Eli had disappeared. Sunny weather didn't mean that a storm wasn't on the horizon. Kane would be watching for it, and he'd be praying that when it hit, they'd all survive.

FIFTEEN

Four double-chocolate chocolate chip cookies was two cookies too many, but Maggie didn't care. She bit into her fourth cookie with as much enjoyment as she had the first, savoring the rich chocolatey taste as Kane and Eli battled aliens on a computer screen. For the first time in days, she felt completely relaxed, and she savored that as much as she did the cookie.

"Want a cup of coffee or a glass of milk?" Kane's mother asked from her seat in a rocking chair. Slim and young looking, Lila Dougherty had the kind of easygoing nature that could make anyone feel welcome. Her husband, Richard, and daughter, Jenna, were just as warm and hospitable.

And Maggie did feel welcome.

So welcome she was tempted to stay exactly where she was, sitting on the sofa in Kane's living room, a warm fire crackling in the fireplace, laughter and conversation swirling around her.

But she'd been there almost three hours, and it was time to go, no matter how much she didn't want to face her silent apartment and her fears. "No, thank you. I need to head home."

"Can't you stay for dinner?" Eli asked, not even glancing

away from the television screen and the giant green monster he was trying to defeat.

"We'd love to have you, Maggie," Lila said, looking up from the quilt she was hand stitching with a beautiful star pattern. "I have a pot roast in the slow cooker, and there's plenty."

"I wish I could, but I have a lot of studying to do. College finals are coming up, and I want to do well." Everything she said was true, but Maggie had been studying consistently. She knew the material, and taking an evening off wouldn't hurt. Except that staying longer would mean driving home in the dark, getting out of the car in the dark, walking to the house in the dark. Sure, there was a deputy stationed outside Edith's house, but the thought still made her shiver.

"Well, then how about tomorrow night?" Lila placed her sewing on the coffee table and stood.

"I—"

"You may as well say yes. My family is very persistent when they want something." Jenna had been sitting in a chair close to the fire, conversing with everyone, her laughing, animated expression in sharp contrast to her pale fragility.

"Persistent? More like doggedly driven." Kane set the game control down and stretched, his T-shirt pulling against firm biceps and hard abs.

Maggie looked away, her cheeks heating, her pulse racing.

Physical attraction. That was all it was.

Or all she wanted it to be.

Because that she could deal with. That she could ignore.

What she couldn't ignore was the way she felt when she looked into Kane's eyes. He knew about her past, knew about her mistakes, but he still looked at her as if she were the most beautiful woman in the world, treated her as if she were the kind of woman she'd always longed to be.

"I'll make chicken and dumplings, and we can have warm pecan pie and ice cream for dessert. I used to be a Southern girl, you know." Lila smiled winningly, and Maggie saw Eli in her pale skin and freckled face.

Maggie smiled. "No, I didn't know that."

"It's true. Southern through and through until I met Richard on a mission trip to Mexico City. He was a Yankee, but I forgave him."

"After you made me promise that we'd never live north of the Mason-Dixon Line." Richard slid an arm around his wife's waist and pulled her close. More than six feet tall with a runner's build and the same clear green eyes as his son, he seemed quiet and steady, a man who could be depended on.

Like Kane.

"Yet somehow we ended up in New York." Lila feigned a disgusted sigh. "Which just goes to show that God's plans are often much different than our own. Now, how about dinner tomorrow? Richard and I are leaving Saturday, and we'd love to see you one more time before we go."

"I…" Maggie knew she should say no. She even felt the word forming on her tongue. Somehow it never made it out of her mouth. "Sure. I'd love to join you for dinner tomorrow night. I'll bring the ice cream to go with the pie."

"Wonderful!" Lila grabbed Maggie's hand and pulled her into a hug that was as easy and comfortable as it was unexpected.

"She's not going to be able to come tomorrow if you don't let her leave today, Mom." Jenna's wry comment made Maggie smile as she stepped away from Lila.

"Here's your coat. I put something in the pocket. A

little snack for later." Richard handed Maggie her coat and winked.

"Thank you, Mr. Dougherty."

"Richard."

"I'm going to escort Maggie to her place. I'll be back in half an hour." Kane's words were like a splash of ice water in her face, and all the warmth Maggie had been feeling, all the contentment and peace fled. Derrick was in Deer Park. For all she knew, he was outside Kane's house, just waiting to shoot whoever walked out the door first.

"Kane, that's not necessary. Stay here with your family. I'll be fine." And if she ran into Derrick, at least she wouldn't take someone else down with her.

"You know I'm not going to do that, right?" he murmured, as he pulled the edges of her coat together and lifted the collar to cover her ears, his knuckles brushing the tender flesh beneath her jaw.

She shivered, knowing she should step away but stepped closer instead. "It would be better if you did."

"You may as well not argue, Maggie. You're not going to win." Jenna spoke into the tension, her easy grin doing nothing to ease Maggie's fear or slow her racing pulse.

"Can I come, too?" Eli asked, and Maggie and Kane both said no, their voices merging and overlapping, so that they could easily have been one. In agreement. For once.

"Why not?"

"Because you were supposed to show me how to fight aliens," Lila responded. He frowned but didn't argue.

"I'll see you all tomorrow night. I have a class from three to five. Is six too late to come by?"

"Six is perfect." Lila offered another smile, and Maggie couldn't help wondering what it would have been like to be raised by a woman like her. A woman of faith and conviction and easy good humor, one who put the needs of her family before her own needs. Not a perfect mother, but a loving one.

If Maggie were ever to get married and have kids, that's the kind of mother she'd want to be. The kind of *person* she'd want to be.

Married? With kids?

No way was that going to happen.

Maggie had made that decision years ago.

But, then, she'd also decided to live a party life, to give herself over to the same addiction and sin her mother and grandmother had fallen into.

And here she was in a small town, living a clean, God-honoring life, doing her best to be the kind of person He wanted her to be.

Which just goes to show that God's plans are often much different than our own.

Lila's words seemed to echo through Maggie's mind as she followed Kane out the front door.

"I'll be right behind you all the way to your place. When we get there, don't get out of your car until I come open the door, okay?" There was a hard edge to Kane's voice, and Maggie nodded, looking up into his face and seeing the determination there.

"Kane, I really wish you'd stay here. Eli needs a father, and I couldn't live with myself if Derrick took that from him."

"Derrick is after you, not me. And based on the crimes he's committed so far, I'd say he prefers to make things look like an accident. He won't use a gun or a knife, and he won't strike when there are witnesses around. He'll wait until he thinks no one is looking. Then he'll pounce."

"That's...comforting." She shuddered at the thought of Derrick lurking in the shadows waiting for just the right opportunity to attack.

Kane smiled gently and ran his knuckle along her cheek, the touch tender and light. "It's going to be okay, Maggie."

"I hope you're right."

"How can I not be? God is in control. He's performed miracles already, and I don't think He plans to stop until He sees us through this."

Maggie tried to believe that as she got in her car and pulled out onto the road. She *did* believe it, but she was terrified anyway. Terrified of Derrick and of what she knew he was capable of. Terrified of her fickle heart and the way it leaped and jumped whenever Kane was around. Terrified of losing what she had, but even more terrified of keeping it and missing out on what she might gain if only she were willing to relax and let God lead where He would.

The sedan was still parked in front of Edith's house when Maggie pulled into the driveway, but she stayed in her car anyway, waiting as Kane knocked on Edith's door. It swung open, and Kane jogged to Maggie's car.

"Ready?" he asked as she opened the door.

"Sure."

"Then let's go." He offered a hand, and she accepted, allowing his support as he helped her from the car. His arm slid around her waist, and he positioned her so that her back was to his chest, his body shielding hers from the street. His warmth enveloped her. His scent surrounded her. Masculine and strong and so compelling she wanted to lean into it, lean into him.

Her heart slammed against her chest as she and Kane moved in tandem up the driveway, onto the porch and into the house. As soon as they crossed the threshold, Kane closed the door, then took a step away. "You're not going anywhere tonight, are you?"

"Of course she's not, and if she tries, I'm going to hog-tie her like I used to do with my kids when they were being ornery." Edith hovered in the threshold of the living room, her face creased with concern.

"You did not hog-tie your children," Maggie responded, more because it was expected than because she wanted to engage in conversation.

"No, but I will hog-tie *you*, so don't tempt me to do it. You go up to that apartment, and you stay there until the sun is up."

"I will. Good night, Edith."

"Good night, my dear." Edith disappeared back into the living room, and Maggie started up the stairs, not even bothering to tell Kane not to follow. He would. She knew it, and the knowledge filled her with warmth.

He put his hand on hers as she unlocked the door, stopping her before she opened it. "Let me. Just in case."

"In case what? Derrick would have had to bypass a deputy, climb a two-story building and open a locked window to get in there." But Maggie stepped aside anyway, letting Kane open the door and step into the apartment ahead of her.

"Mind if I take a look down the hall?" he asked, already moving in that direction.

"Kane, I really don't think this is necessary." She followed him into her room, nearly walking into his back when he stopped to survey the small, sparsely furnished area. "See? There's nowhere for anyone to hide."

"How about a closet?"

"I use the wardrobe." She gestured to the large oak wardrobe that Edith had placed against the far wall.

"Do you mind?"

She shook her head, and Kane opened the wardrobe, glancing inside as if he really thought Derrick might have managed to enter Maggie's house and hide there.

"You can check under the bed, too, if you want," Maggie said, and Kane shot a quick grin in her direction.

"I planned on it. I figured that would save you some time later."

"Later?"

"Yeah. When it's quiet and late, and you can't sleep, you may start wondering if Lyons somehow snuck in. If I check now, you won't have to later." He made a show of checking under the bed, then stepped past Maggie and back out into the hall.

She followed him to the bathroom, standing in the doorway as he checked behind the shower curtain.

"That's it. Looks like the apartment is clear." He walked back out into the living room.

"Did you really think it wouldn't be?"

"No, but acting like I did gave me a good excuse to spend a little time alone with you." He wrapped his arms around her waist and tugged her close. She could feel his warmth, smell the spicy scent of his aftershave.

"If that's what you wanted, you could have just said so."

"If I had, you would have sent me on my way, and then I couldn't have done this." He dropped a kiss on her forehead. "Or this." Dropped another one on her cheek. "Or this." The last landed on the corner of her mouth, and Maggie's pulse leaped.

"So you were just plotting to steal kisses?" Her voice was raspy with longing, and she knew she should step out of his arms, refuse what she was feeling.

But being with Kane felt more right than anything had in a very long time, and she stayed where she was.

"I'm not stealing. I'm giving. Consider them a thank-you. I had a great time with you tonight, Maggie. My whole family did," he murmured, his lips brushing the tender flesh behind her ear.

She shivered, leaning in close, giving in to the moment.

"I had a great time with all of you, too."

"Good, because I'd like to repeat the experience many times in the future."

"Your parents will be going home soon."

"True, and I'll miss them, but I don't think we need them around to have fun. Although, my father did add a little something special to the night."

"What's that?"

"He made you smell like chocolate."

"Chocolate?"

"I figured it was the bag of cookies he shoved in your coat pocket. But maybe it's just you. I've always had a weak spot for chocolate, you know." He smiled, cupping her face in his hands, his eyes the soft green of distant mountains, the tenderness in his gaze so real that Maggie could feel it to the very depth of her soul.

It made her weak and vulnerable and all the things she knew she didn't want to be, but she still didn't step out of his arms. "Kane... I'm not sure this is a good idea."

"Funny, I was just thinking what a great idea it is." His lips brushed the corner of her mouth again, hesitated there.

Maybe he was waiting for Maggie to move away.

Maybe he was giving her a chance to prove what a bad idea it really was.

But she didn't. Couldn't. His lips touched hers sweetly, gently, as if he were afraid of scaring her away. Afraid to end what had barely begun.

It wasn't their first kiss, but the emotion behind it cut a

knife through Maggie's heart, left it raw and wounded and open.

Tears slid down her cheeks, but she didn't care; she couldn't care about anything but Kane and the power of his embrace.

His hands slipped from her face, rested on her shoulders as he looked down into her eyes.

"I've made you cry again." He brushed a tear away with his thumb, kissed the spot where it had been. "Why?"

"Maybe because when I'm with you I feel like the person I've always wanted to be." Her voice broke, and Kane pulled her into his arms, offering a hug that gave everything and demanded nothing.

"You've always been that person, Maggie. It just took you a while to find her." He stepped back again, his face tight with emotion. "I need to go. Be careful tomorrow, Maggie. Don't take any chances when you go out."

"I won't." Somehow she managed to speak, to walk with Kane as he opened the door and stepped out of the apartment.

And somehow she managed to say goodbye, to act as if her entire world hadn't just shifted, as if her focus hadn't just completely changed.

She'd spent years living her life, never once allowing herself to dream of all the things she'd given up on when she was too young and foolish to realize how important they were.

Marriage, kids, Christmases with noise and laughter, Thanksgivings around large tables filled to capacity. Those were the things she'd wanted before she'd decided that a party life would be more fun.

She closed the door, then leaned her back against it as if locking Kane out could change the way he'd made her feel.

"*What am I going to do, Lord? What should I do?*" she prayed as she moved away from the door.

She wanted an answer, maybe an audible voice as God provided clear direction, but she got nothing.

"Well, at least I have cookies." She pulled the bag from her pocket and bit into her fifth cookie of the day. It tasted like chalk in her mouth, and she shoved half of it back in the bag.

Chocolate could cure a lot of ills, but it couldn't find Derrick and put him in jail, and it couldn't help Maggie figure out what was going on between herself and Kane.

What was going on?

She knew what was going on. Kane had stepped over the line from friendship into something more, and she'd stepped over it with him. Willingly. Happily.

And she should regret it, but she didn't.

Did she?

She was too tired to know, too scared, too worried about what tomorrow would bring. Derrick was in Deer Park, and eventually he'd do what he'd come to do.

All she should be thinking about, all she should be worried about was surviving.

SIXTEEN

Maggie had loved college from the day she'd gotten up the nerve to enroll and walk onto the Eastern Washington State University campus. Each class was an accomplishment, and every credit she earned was a step closer to her goal of obtaining a teaching degree. With finals coming up, she couldn't afford to be distracted or overtired, but she was both as she sat through her Curriculum and the Elementary Classroom course.

She stifled a yawn as the professor dismissed class, then she stood with the rest of the students. They poured out into the hall, but Maggie followed more slowly. She'd stayed in her apartment all day, then hurried to her car an hour before class, her heart pounding and her stomach churning with fear. Still, she hadn't actually expected Derrick to be waiting for her outside Edith's house, not with a patrol car stationed in front of the house.

No. He'd wait until she wasn't expecting it. Wait until he was sure he wouldn't be caught and stopped. Just as Kane had said.

Outside, darkness had descended, and Maggie hesitated at the door of the humanities building. There were still plenty of people milling around, but that wasn't as comforting as Maggie wanted it to be. For all she knew, Derrick was one of the people out there. For all she knew, he was waiting near her car, hoping for an opportunity to drag her away.

And she knew what would happen if he did.

She knew how it would end.

Derrick didn't make idle threats. She'd known that before Kane had told her about the three women who'd died after dating Derrick. She'd known it, but she'd hoped she was wrong. Hoped that maybe he really had forgotten her and moved on.

She pulled out her cell phone and dialed the sheriff's office. Maybe something had happened in the last few hours. Maybe they'd tracked down Derrick and thrown him in jail.

It took her less than five minutes to confirm what she'd already known. Derrick was still on the loose. The Miami police had contacted several small airports in the area, and they suspected that Derrick had hired a private plane to carry him across the country.

They were a day late and a dollar short with the information. Not that knowing it any sooner would have changed things. The die had been cast the day Maggie went to the sheriff with information about Eli. Nothing could have changed what had happened since then.

She sighed, pushing open the door and stepping into the cold night, her cell phone still clutched in her hand. The area was well lit, and she jogged to her car and fumbled with her keys, shaking as she got in and slammed the door shut again.

The cell phone rang as she shoved the keys into the ignition, and Maggie screamed, dropping the phone and then scrambling to pick it up again.

"Hello?"

"Hey, it's me."

Maggie knew the warm baritone, could picture Kane standing in his living room, a fire crackling behind him. "Kane. I didn't realize you had my cell phone number."

"Is that the same as, 'I wish you didn't have my cell phone number'?" he asked, and Maggie could hear the smile in his voice. She'd spent the better part of twenty-four hours trying to put Kane out of her mind, trying to forget the way she'd felt when she'd been in his arms.

She'd failed, and her skipping, dancing heart was proof of it. "No, I'm just surprised."

"I called Edith, and she gave me the number. I wanted to check in and see if you were still planning to come for dinner tonight."

"I'll be there. I'm just going to go back to my place and grab the ice cream Edith picked up for me earlier."

"Just be careful, Maggie. I don't want anything to happen to you."

"That makes two of us." She tried to laugh, but it came out flat and hard.

"Your class is over, right?"

"Yes, I'm leaving now."

"Call security. Ask for an escort to your car."

"I'm already in my car. I'll be home in a half hour, and at your place by six."

"You walked to your car without an escort?"

"The same way I do every night."

"But this isn't every night, Maggie. This is a night when you know that your ex-boyfriend is coming after you." He was right, of course, but Maggie wasn't sure she appreciated the hard edge to his voice.

"I'm an adult, Kane. I think I'm aware of the kind of trouble I'm in."

"Then promise me you won't go anywhere without an escort from now on."

Promise?

It seemed so simple, but Maggie didn't believe in making promises she couldn't keep, and she wasn't sure she could keep that one. "That might be difficult. I have to live my life. No matter where Derrick is or what he's planning."

"Putting your life on hold for a few days makes more sense than losing it."

"I'm not planning to lose it."

"No, but Lyons is planning to take it. And I'm worried about you." His tone had softened, filled with concern, and Maggie softened with it.

"I'll be careful. I *can* promise you that."

"Good, I'll see you in about forty minutes."

"See you then." She hung up, shoving the phone in her pocket and starting the car engine.

She had expected a lot of things to happen when she decided to go to the sheriff with her suspicions about Eli. She'd expected she might be in the news and that Derrick might find her. She'd expected to be in danger. She'd even expected to leave Deer Park for good. What she hadn't expected was to find something she'd given up dreaming of.

And she had.

If she could only allow herself to believe in it.

You already do.

Maybe, but she was afraid, too. Worried that if she wanted it too much, grabbed it too tightly, the dream would slip through her fingers and disappear like mist on a mountain lake.

Whatever your plans, Lord, whatever your dreams for my life, I'm open to them. Just show me the way you want me to go. Show me the right choices to make.

She sighed, pulling into Edith's driveway, the darkness pressing in around the Ford as Maggie turned off the ignition. A dark sedan was parked across the street, and Edith had left the porch light on. Its golden glow should have been comforting. Instead, it cast long shadows that twisted and twined into faceless, shapeless forms.

Was someone hiding near the edge of the porch?

Were black eyes gleaming out at her from the darkness?

Of course not. If someone were out there the deputy would have spotted him by now. Still, Maggie tensed, searching the shadows for movement. She saw nothing, heard nothing as she opened the door and eased out into the night. Keys clutched in her hand, she ran the few yards to the porch, shoved her keys in the lock and opened the door. The foyer was dark, the light in the living room off. Surprised, Maggie peeked into the room but, saw no sign of her landlady.

"Edith? You around?" she called out, walking into Edith's dining room, then her kitchen. It was too early for Edith to have retired for the night, but it was possible she'd gone out with friends. Widowed at a young age, Edith had spent years raising her children. Now that they were grown and gone, she had an active life filled with friends.

Still, Maggie's uneasiness didn't leave, and she walked down a short hall to Edith's bedroom suite. "Edith?"

She knocked on the door. Heard nothing.

"Okay, so she's out for the evening. She's out more than she's home, so stop overreacting, get the ice cream and get ready to go to Kane's," Maggie said as she turned and heard something creak in the room above her head.

Her room.

Maggie froze, then backed away from Edith's door, ears straining to hear more above the harsh beat of her heart.

Another creak.

A soft shuffling.

Footsteps. Slow. Deliberate. Moving across the floor above her head.

Maggie's blood went cold, and she ran for the front door, her breath coming fast and hard. She needed to get out, call the police.

She grabbed the door handle, her palm slippery against the metal as she turned it, then felt the cold sweep of winter air as it blew into the house.

"Going somewhere, Angel?"

The name.

The voice.

The life Maggie had managed to outrun for three years had finally caught up to her.

She didn't turn. Didn't want to see Derrick standing at the top of the stairs, didn't want to look into his cold, dark eyes.

"You can keep going if you want. Keep on running, and I'll keep on finding you. Of course, with you gone, I'll have to spend my time with someone else. That nice landlady of yours'll do. We've been having a good conversation while we waited for you to show up. It's a shame the cop couldn't join in, but he was otherwise engaged."

His words filled Maggie with dread, and she knew she had no choice but to turn around and look Derrick in the eyes.

"Where is Edith? What did you do to her? What did you do to the deputy?"

"Nothing permanent. Yet. The cop, he'll live. Unless that knock on the head scrambled his brains more than it should have. Come morning, his replacement will find him trussed up like the pig he is, lying behind some bushes in the yard. Your friend? What happens to her is up to you." He smiled, his straight white teeth gleaming in his deeply tanned face.

"If you hurt her—"

"What? What are you going to do? Nothing. That's what, because you're weak and stupid and not worth the time and the effort I put into finding you." He spat the words out, the ugliness of them the slap in the face Maggie needed to start thinking again. Moving again.

"I want to see her."

"You don't get a say in what happens from now on, Angel. It's all about me and what I want."

"What do you want?"

"A little bit of time, that's all. We didn't exactly get to say goodbye when you left Miami."

"We said goodbye months before I actually left Florida. About five minutes after you beat me senseless."

"The way I remember it, you walked out on me. Then you went to the police and lied about me and my business. Caused me thousands of dollars and a lot of hours. You owe me."

"So give me a bill, and I'll pay."

"Do you really think I'd make it so easy for you, Angel?" He smiled and crooked a finger. "You're looking good, babe. Better than you did three years ago. Come on up here. Give me the kind of hello I like."

"I'll do whatever you say *after* I see Edith. I want to make sure she's okay."

"You really think I'd hurt an old lady?"

"You hurt me."

"You weren't an old lady. You were a snotty little witch who thought she could tell me what was what. I bet you've changed, though, haven't you? I bet you realize how good you had it when you were with me." His eyes were wild, and Maggie wondered if he was on something.

She took a deep breath and tried to clear her head. She

needed to think, not panic. That was the only way she was going to keep Edith and herself alive.

"You always took good care of me, Derrick," she offered, the words rasping out past her dry throat. She needed him to relax his guard, to begin to believe that he had the upper hand.

"You're right. And how did you repay me, huh? How? I'll tell you how, you lied about me. Tried to get me thrown in jail, but it didn't work, did it?"

"No." It was all she could manage. Derrick *was* high on something. Knowing him, he'd taken a few hits of cocaine, and it was speeding through his blood, making him even more dangerous than usual.

"Because you're stupid, Angel. That's why. You don't know squat about anything. Now, get up here. We've got some unfinished business to take care of."

She didn't want to. She wanted to turn around and run out the door, but that would mean leaving Edith, and she couldn't do that.

"Come on. Hurry it up, or you'll make me mad. You don't want to do that, do you?"

"No." She moved reluctantly, her body shaking with a fear she didn't dare acknowledge. If she did, she'd collapse into a puddle on the floor, and any hope of escape would be lost.

As soon as she reached the top step, Derrick lunged, grabbing her by the throat and slamming her up against the wall. She saw stars and felt herself sliding into darkness.

"What? You don't fight anymore?"

She heard his voice through a haze of pain, and she struggled to keep her grip on consciousness. "I've changed."

"Changed? No one changes, Angel. Not for real, anyway." He dragged her away from the wall and pulled her so close she could feel the heat of his body and smell the putrid scent of his breath. She gagged, her stomach heaving as Derrick shoved her in through the open door of the apartment.

She stumbled, landing on her hands and knees and scrambling to get back on her feet.

The door slammed, the lock turned and the world went silent as Derrick stalked toward her, lithe and dangerous. Five years ago, she'd fallen hard for those things, never noticing the darkness in his eyes, the wildness.

"It's finally just the two of us again. I've been waiting a long time for this, Angel. A long time." He ran a finger down her cheek, and she shuddered.

"Please, let me check on Edith. Let me make sure she's okay."

"I told you she was. Isn't my word good enough for you?"

Maggie recognized the sharp tone, the tightening fists. He could knock her down and out with one blow, and she'd be no good to Edith or to herself.

"It is, but Edith has a heart condition, and she's not strong. Too much stress could kill her," she lied, praying that it would work.

"She's fine." Derrick dragged Maggie into his arms, tried to pull her close.

"I can't." She shoved away, moving back, trying to smile past her terror. "I'm too worried. You know how I am. You know I can't stand to think of an older person hurting. It reminds me too much of my grandmother." That much was true, and Maggie hoped that Derrick would see that through his drug-dazed brain.

He stared at her for a moment, his eyes hard and hot and angry, and then he shrugged, grabbing her upper arm and squeezing hard as he dragged her down the hall and into her room.

Edith was there, tied up in a chair Derrick must have dragged from the dining room, her mouth covered with duct tape, her eyes wide with terror. "Edith, are you okay?"

Maggie tried to cross the room, but Derrick dragged her back. "She's fine, and she'll stay that way as long as you do exactly what I say. You hear me?"

"Yes."

"Good. We're going to walk down the stairs. We're going to get in your car, and we're going to leave town."

"Where are we going?"

"For a ride."

She needed to get more information now, while Edith was listening. "To a hotel?"

"To a friend's place. He's got a nice little setup in the mountains, and I think we'll be plenty cozy there."

It wasn't much to go on, but Maggie didn't have a chance to ask more. Derrick yanked her back out the door and shoved her into the living room. "You stay here while I take care of Grandma."

"What do you mean?"

"Just what I said." He turned to walk down the hall, and Maggie threw herself at his legs, hoping to bring him down.

He went, falling with a crash that seemed to shake the house.

She tried to run down the hall and into the bedroom, but he grabbed her ankle and yanked hard.

Maggie screamed as she fell, her head slamming into the wall. For a moment she knew nothing, and then Derrick's hands wrapped around her throat, tightening, and she knew she had to fight or die.

She tried to scream as she clawed at his hands, tried to loosen his grip.

Please, God. I don't want to die. I don't want Edith to die. Please, help us.

The prayer welled up from the deepest part of her soul, welled out and filled her head until she could hear nothing else. Not Derrick's panting breaths, not her pulsing blood, not the frantic throb of her terror.

Somewhere in the distance a phone rang, the sound seeping into Maggie's mind, drawing her attention. It must have drawn Derrick's, too. His grip loosened, and Maggie was able to twist away and stand up. The phone continued to ring. Not her home phone, her cell phone, which was still in her back pocket.

"It's my friend. If I don't pick up, he'll come looking for me," she rasped out, wondering if it was true. If Kane really could be calling.

"Friend? You mean that guy who was over here last night? Guy whose kid you found?" Derrick blinked, seeming to come out of the rage that had nearly gotten Maggie killed.

"Yes."

"Let him come. I can deal with him."

"But he'll bring the sheriff with him. They know you're in town, and if they can't contact me, they'll assume it's because of you."

He frowned, then nodded. "Okay, answer it, but you say anything I don't like and I'll march into the bedroom and wring your friend's neck."

He would. Maggie knew it.

She pulled the phone from her pocket, her hand shaking as she pushed talk.

Please, God, let it be Kane. Please let him understand that I need help.

She pressed it to her ear and tried to speak. Failed.

"Hello? Maggie?" It *was* Kane, his voice anchoring her

to reality, reminding her that she wasn't Angel Simmons anymore. Reminding her that she wasn't alone. That there were people who cared, who'd help.

"I'm here."

"Are you home or still on the road?"

"Home."

"Great. How about I come pick you up?"

"That's not necessary."

"Maybe not, but it'll make me feel better. I know there's a deputy outside Edith's house, but anything could happen between there and here."

"Something already has," she said, her gaze shooting to Derrick. He frowned and moved a step closer.

"What?" The alarm in Kane's voice was obvious, and Maggie wondered if Derrick could hear it.

"Finish the conversation. Now!" Derrick hissed, and Maggie had no choice but to obey.

"I won't be able to make it tonight. I've got too much to do before I return to school on Monday."

"You mean for college?"

"No, for Eli's class. I've got grading and stuff to do." She shot another quick glance in Derrick's direction. He was losing patience, and she was running out of time.

"You're going back to work?"

"On Monday. Just like I was planning."

"I see. My parents will be disappointed to not see you again before they leave, but I'll explain things to them."

"Okay."

"I'd better let you get back to work. I'll see you at church Sunday." Did he not get it? Did he not understand that Maggie wouldn't be seeing anyone again unless help arrived fast?

"All right. Goodbye."

"Bye." He hung up, and Maggie didn't have the heart

to end the call, to cut off the only connection she had with safety.

"Good job, Angel. Maybe I'll let your friend live after all." Derrick smiled, the ugly, evil look in his eyes saying something entirely different.

"You said we were going to go to your friend's in the mountains."

"We've got time, so how about you make me a sandwich and we'll discuss all the different ways you can pay for your friend's life?" He dropped down onto the sofa, put his feet on the coffee table and stared Maggie down.

Whatever drug he'd taken had scrambled his thinking. He wanted to be served, and he wanted her to do the serving. In his mind that equated to power and powerlessness, and that was all he seemed to care about.

In Maggie's mind, it was a reprieve, a little extra time to think and to plan.

"I could make you some soup, too. I have tomato or clam chowder."

"You know I love chowder. Make me that and the sandwich, and then we'll work out that payment plan. And don't try anything funny."

"I won't."

Unless she could think of something that would work.

She hurried into the kitchen, her hands shaking as she pulled out the can of soup and got to work.

SEVENTEEN

Kane kept his headlights off as he parked a few houses away from Edith's place. The dark sedan was exactly where it had been for the past twenty-four hours, but Kane doubted a deputy was in it. He wasn't sure how Derrick had managed it, but he breached security and was inside Edith's house. God willing, he hadn't killed anyone to get there. God willing, he wouldn't kill anyone to escape. The sheriff's cruiser was parked in a driveway across the street, and Kane was sure there were other police cars and officers close by. He doubted any of them would be happy that he was there, but he didn't care. Maggie was in trouble. He'd heard it in her voice the moment she'd answered the phone. He had wanted to tell her he understood and that help was on the way. He hadn't been able to, of course. Not without cluing Lyons in and ruining the element of surprise.

Adrenaline pumping, Kane opened his car door, easing out into the darkness and sliding into the shadows. The air seemed thick with expectancy, the night too silent and still. A shadow broke away from a small cove of trees, stepping toward Kane as he approached Edith's house.

"What are you doing here, Dougherty?" the sheriff asked in a whisper that carried through the darkness.

"The same thing you are. Saving Maggie."

"We have things under control. Adding a civilian into the mix is a potential hazard that I'm not willing to risk. Go back to your car. Stay there until further notice."

"This isn't the military, Sheriff, and I'm not one of your men."

"If you care about Maggie, you'll act like you are."

"And do what?"

"Stay out of the way."

"I'll be out of the way. I can assure you of that." But he wouldn't be in the car. He was going to walk the perimeter of the house and see if he could find a way in.

"Look, Dougherty, I know you're concerned, and I know you want to help. I even know that in your position, I'd be doing the same, but it's too dangerous for everyone if I include you in this rescue operation."

"How are you planning on getting Maggie and Lyons out?" Kane asked, completely ignoring the sheriff's comments. There was no way he was going to leave without knowing exactly what the plan was.

"I'm sending someone to the door to ring the bell, hoping Maggie will come to open it with Lyons. If he does, I've got a sharpshooter ready to take him out."

"If he doesn't take Maggie out first."

"We can't know for sure that he hasn't already done that. We've got an officer down with a severe head injury. Anything could have happened inside that house." It was true, but Kane didn't want to hear it. Didn't even want to contemplate the idea.

"I spoke to Maggie less than fifteen minutes ago, and she was fine."

"A lot can happen in fifteen minutes."

Kane knew that better than anyone else, and his muscles tightened, his heart pounding a heavy beat. "I'll ring the doorbell."

"It's too risky. You move the wrong way, and you may be the one lying dead instead of Lyons. The best thing you can do is get in your car and wait."

"I have no intention of getting between Lyons and a gun." He walked toward Edith's house, completely ignoring the sheriff's protest until the other man grabbed his arm and yanked him to a stop.

"I can't allow a civilian to get involved in this."

"Do you really think Lyons isn't going to recognize a cop when he sees one? He's a career criminal, a man who's spent his life avoiding the consequences of his behavior."

"We'll take him out long before he realizes we're there."

"And that'll be a lot easier to do if you'll let me go in. I'll ring the doorbell. Maggie will answer it. She knows me, and if Lyons has been watching her for the past few days, he'll have seen me, too. Neither will suspect that I brought police officers with me, and that'll put you at the advantage."

The sheriff frowned and ran a hand down his jaw, his gaze on Edith's house. "I'm not sure I like the idea, but I think it might work. Give me three minutes to communicate with my men. Then ring the doorbell. Once the door opens, see if you can get Maggie to step out onto the porch. That'll give our sharpshooters an easier shot at anyone in the house."

"Will do." Kane glanced at his watch, then waited a minute. Two. Adrenaline and fear made him want to forget waiting, forget everything but getting into the house and freeing Maggie.

At the three-minute mark he walked to the door, then rang the doorbell, praying the plan would work.

A minute passed, and the door remained closed. Kane

rang the doorbell again, pushing so hard that the peal repeated for several seconds.

Inside the house the foyer light came on, and Kane braced himself. *Please, God, let this work.*

A shadow passed in front of the window to the left of the door, and a bolt slid open. Finally, the door cracked open and Maggie's pale face and deep-blue eyes stared out at him.

"Kane! What are you doing here?" Her voice was raspy and dry, and even the dim foyer light couldn't hide the blue smudges on her neck and jaw.

She was bruised. Terrified. But she was alive, and Kane had every intention of making sure she stayed that way.

"Hoping to convince you to have dinner with my family." *Come on. Open the door a little more. Give them a clear shot at anyone who might be standing behind you.*

"I can't, but thank you. It means a lot that you'd want me to be there."

"This is about what happened last night, isn't it?" he asked, pulling at straws, desperate to get the door opened wider.

"Last night?"

"The kiss."

"Kane, I have a lot more on my mind than a kiss."

"Why don't you come out on the porch and tell me about it?"

"I can't. I have to go. Give Eli my love, okay?" There were tears in her eyes and in her voice, and Kane knew she was going to close the door.

"Wait." He slammed his hand against it, keeping it open.

"I really have to go. I'm exhausted and I've got a lot to do between now and Monday."

"Understood, but it wouldn't hurt to spend a few minutes

with a friend, would it?" He stepped close to the door and looked down into Maggie's eyes. She blinked and seemed to see him for the first time since she'd opened the door.

"I—"

"It'll be okay. I promise." He smiled and eased his foot into the opening of the door. Maggie wasn't going to open the door wider, that much was for sure. So he'd either have to walk away and wait for the sheriff to come up with a new plan, or he'd have to take matters into his own hands and pray that it worked out.

He took a deep breath and knew what he had to do.

Then he took a step back, lifted his foot and slammed it into the door, grabbing Maggie's shoulder as she fell backward and shoving her to the side as a figure lunged toward them. Kane caught a glimpse of shiny metal, saw a knife blade slice the air inches from his face and heard Maggie scream.

A shot rang out, but Lyons kept coming, the knife raised, a snarl twisting his features so that he looked nothing like the photos Kane had seen of him.

Kane dodged to the left, colliding with Maggie as she dove to the right. He wrapped an arm around her waist, swinging her around and out of the way as Lyons attacked again.

Kane grabbed his wrist, twisting it up behind his back, trying to get him to loosen his grip on the knife, but Lyons was just as determined to keep it. He twisted out from Kane's hold and turned to face him, a cold, hard smile on his face.

"So, you're the guy Angel thought she'd replace me with. Too bad I don't want to be replaced."

"Too bad you don't have a choice," Kane responded, dodging the knife blade again and wondering what was taking the sheriff so long.

"Sure I do. I kill you. I get the gal. It's as simple as that."

"It would be if I planned to let you kill me."

"Too bad you don't have a choice." Lyons sneered, lunging forward and plunging the knife toward Kane's chest.

He dodged again, knowing the door was still wide open, knowing that Lyons was standing in front of it. This time, he pulled Maggie with him, tackling her to the ground, holding her there as a volley of shots split the night.

Maggie screamed and screamed again, her body trembling as Lyons crumbled onto the floor, blood pooling beneath him.

And then there was silence, so thick and deep Kane wondered if it would ever be broken.

A voice called from outside, and Kane shifted, lifting his weight so that Maggie could move again. He helped her sit up, cupping her face in his hands, looking into her eyes. "Are you okay?"

"I think so."

Footsteps sounded on the porch, and Kane stood, offering Maggie a hand.

And suddenly Lyons was moving again, lunging forward, the knife in his hand, slicing an arch through the air, aiming for Maggie as he crumbled to the ground again.

Maggie stumbled—and fell to her knees.

"Maggie!" Kane scooped her into his arms, backing up as a half dozen deputies raced into the room. She was limp in his arms, her eyes closed, her skin parchment pale.

"Maggie? Can you hear me?"

She opened her eyes and offered a wane smile. "You're screaming in my ear. How could I not?"

"Did he cut you?"

"Barely. Put me down, and you can see for yourself."

He set her on her feet, keeping his hands on her waist

to steady her as he looked at the ragged rip in her coat. It stretched from shoulder to waist, and Kane gently pulled the fabric away, wincing as he saw blood bubbling up from the wound.

"It looks like the blade caught your shoulder, but only got the coat farther down."

"How bad is it?"

"You're going to need stitches."

"Good. I'll have matching scars then. One from the bullet. One from the knife." She smiled, but her lips were trembling.

"They'll only add to your beauty."

"Beauty? I'm a mess."

"You're lovely." He kissed her gently, smiling when her cheeks turned pink.

"That's better."

"What?"

"You were so pale I thought you might pass out. Now you've got a little color in your cheeks."

"And that's how you put color in a woman's cheeks? You kiss her?"

"Not every woman. Just you."

She blushed again, her cheeks deepening to dark rose. "We'd better go free Edith. She's tied up in a chair in my bedroom."

She glanced at Derrick, who lay facedown on the floor, a deputy holding a wad of cloth to his gunshot wound. "I hope he doesn't get up again. That was like one of those horror flicks where the bad guy never stays down."

"You don't have to worry. He won't be coming after you again." The sheriff appeared at her side, his concerned gaze taking in the coat Kane held to her shoulder and the bruises on her face and neck.

"Is he..." Maggie didn't finish the thought, but the sheriff must have known what she meant.

"He's alive, but he'll probably wish he weren't after we get through with him."

"Sic Edith on him, and he'll be even sorrier." Maggie shifted again and started toward the stairs. "I need to make sure she's okay."

"I've already sent someone to free her," the sheriff replied. "Just rest there until the ambulance comes."

"Maggie! Maggie Mae Tennyson." Edith's screech carried down the stairs as she was carried out of the apartment by two young deputies. "Are you okay?"

"Yes. I'm fine." Maggie turned to face Edith, swaying a little with the movement. "Are you?"

"Nothing's hurt but my pride. That cad tricked me into letting him in. Said he was delivering flowers for you, and I made the mistake of opening the door. I should have known better."

"How could you have?" Maggie asked as the deputies and Edith reached the bottom of the stairs.

"I don't know, but I do know this. The next time a guy comes up to the door carrying a couple of dozen roses, I'm going to beam him with my frying pan first and ask questions later."

"I guess I'm not going to bring Maggie roses anytime soon," Kane said, urging Maggie to sit on the bottom step while she waited for the ambulance.

"I'll make an exception for you. You did, after all, save her life."

"For the second time," Maggie added, and she smiled into his eyes.

"I'll save it a million times more if that's what it takes."

"For what?"

"For me to show you how much you mean to me."

"You've already done that, Kane." She grabbed his hand, tugging him down to sit beside her and leaning forward to press a kiss to his lips.

"What was that for?"

"It was just to show you how much *you* mean to *me*."

"You've already done that, but feel free to keep demonstrating." She smiled at that, leaning her head against his shoulder and closing her eyes, her warmth seeping through Kane, reminding him that his arms had been empty for much too long.

Now they were filled with Maggie, with Eli, with all the joy and excitement the two brought into his life.

"I love you, Maggie," he whispered in her ear, and she opened her eyes and looked into his face.

"I love you, too."

At her words, all the lonely years, all the years Kane had spent desperately clinging to hope, faded. God had given him a miracle, and then He'd given Kane more.

A double blessing.

A double measure.

A heaping double helping of love.

EPILOGUE

"Are you sure this dress doesn't make me look fat, Maggie Mae?" Edith stood in front of the mirror and patted ample hips encased in sequined peach fabric.

"It makes you look lovely, Edith."

"Lovely and fat. I knew I should have bought another one." She frowned, turning to the left and then to the right, the sequins shimmering in the overhead light of Starr Road Christian Church's choir room.

"And miss a golden opportunity to wear that peach dress?" Jenna stepped up next to Edith and patted the older woman on the back, her dress a simple cream-colored sheath with a peach ribbon at the waist. "Why in the world would you have done that? Besides, Maggie is right. You look great."

"Humph. I'd look a whole lot better if I didn't have to stand up there with you. Stick thin, that's what you are, too beautiful for your own good and five decades younger than me. I'm going to look like an old hag standing next to you."

Jenna smiled. "A hag? Not even close. As for the decades, I don't think either of us look a day over twenty-one." Jenna frowned at her reflection, leaning close to smooth a chin-length strand of red hair from her cheek. Her face had filled out since Maggie had met her the previous fall, but she still looked fragile and gaunt.

"You're both gorgeous, and I don't want to hear another word about that not being true," Maggie said. "Besides, you're hogging the mirror and I need to make sure I look..."

"Perfect?" Edith offered.

"Stunning?" Jenna asked.

"Presentable." Maggie took her place in front of the mirror and smoothed a nonexistent wrinkle from her silk gown.

"Presentable? Presentable is for college graduation. Presentable is for senior photos. Presentable is *not* for the most important day of your life." Edith blinked rapidly, and Maggie was sure there were tears in her eyes.

"Have I told you both how much it means to me to have you standing up for me today?" Maggie asked, clasping hands with both of them and smiling into the mirror.

"And have I told you how much it means to me that you didn't choose one of those horrible tulle gowns for my bridesmaid's dress?" Jenna responded, and Maggie laughed.

"I thought about it. Just to torture you. But then I realized that I'd be torturing myself, too, since I'd have to see it in photos for the rest of my life. Besides, Edith really did want to wear her peach dress." She turned, glancing over her shoulder so she could view the back of the gown. It was elegant and simple, the hand beading at the waist the only ornament. Despite what she'd said about just being presentable, Maggie had to admit she was pleased with the gown and with the cascade of tawny curls that Jenna had created with a curling iron.

"Mom did a beautiful job making your dress. You look stunning." For once, Jenna was serious, her gray-blue eyes skimming over the gown, then resting on Maggie's face. "You really love him, don't you, Mags?"

"I couldn't do this if I didn't. I'd end up being one of those runaway brides, hopping on a horse and riding into the sunset in my beautiful gown." Her hand shook as she twisted the white-gold engagement ring she'd been wearing for six months. She was done running, but she *was* scared.

Scared of the vows she was about to make.

Scared of the commitment.

Scared that somehow she'd mess up and she'd ruin everything.

"Don't be nervous, sweetie. Kane loves you, too. And so does Eli." Jenna squeezed her hand, then stepped away from the mirror and lifted the long-stemmed peach rose she was going to carry down the aisle.

"He's really come far in the past year, hasn't he? I can't believe the young man who celebrated his tenth birthday a few weeks ago is the same scrawny, scared little boy who kicked my behind in Monopoly last Thanksgiving." Edith lifted her own rose, sniffing it delicately. "Lovely."

"You didn't attack the person who delivered it, did you?" Jenna asked, shooting a sly smile in Edith's direction.

"Young lady, I'll have you know that I've not swung my frying pan at anyone in at least a week."

"A week. That's a record." Maggie tried to laugh, but failed miserably.

Should a bride be so nervous on her wedding day?

"You're awfully pale. You're not going to pass out or anything, are you?" Jenna put a hand on Maggie's cheek and frowned.

"Of course not."

"Good because I don't want to have to drag you down the aisle."

"I'm sure if it came down to that, Kane would be happy to fetch his beautiful bride." Edith straightened the ribbon on Maggie's bouquet of white and peach roses and handed it to her. "But it won't. Because Maggie and Kane and Eli belong together, and Maggie knows it, don't you, dear?"

"Of course." And she did know it with every fiber of her being, but she was still scared.

"How could you not?" Edith said, as if Maggie hadn't even spoken. "God doesn't play games, and it was no game when He brought you and Kane together. All that trouble and trial you two went through, and in the midst of it all, you falling in love. That's a miracle, Maggie, and don't you ever forget it."

Edith was right. God *had* performed miracles to bring Maggie and Kane together. And now, with Derrick in prison for murdering three of his girlfriends and Susannah Peyton in jail for kidnapping, they were free to move on with their lives. "I won't."

"Good. That's what I want to hear. Pinch your cheeks to get some color back in them because it's just about time to go."

A soft knock sounded on the door, and Maggie tensed, her stomach fluttering with nerves.

"Just about time? It *is* time!" Jenna hurried to the door, pulled it open and smiled at the handsome young man who stood on the other side of it. "Eli Dougherty, I have never seen you look so handsome."

He blushed, but his gaze was on Maggie, his green eyes filled with the same apprehension she was feeling. During the past few months, he'd opened up about the time he'd spent with Susannah. He'd admitted to calling her Mom and to accepting her as his mother. The guilt he felt over that was something he'd been working hard to overcome, and the success he was having showed in the easy way he communicated with Maggie and with Kane.

Still, he had to go at his own pace in the new relationships they were forming, and Maggie had no intention of asking him to call her Mom, no intention at all of trying to replace the mother he'd lost just a few months after he was born.

But she *would* mother him.

She *would* love him.

She already had.

She already did.

"You do look handsome, Eli," she said, and he blushed again.

"*You* look beautiful."

"Then, I guess we'll be two of the best-looking people walking down the aisle."

Eli smiled at that, then pulled a small box from behind his back.

"I have something for you."

"You do?"

"Yep. I finally beat Grandpa at chess, and he paid me and everything. Just like he said. So I bought this for you. I hope you like it."

"Oh, Eli, you shouldn't have spent your money on me."

Jenna smiled. "But he did, so open the gift before my brother comes looking for you and blames me because you're late." She ruffled Eli's hair and smoothed it down again.

Maggie pulled the pink ribbon from the box and lifted the lid, her eyes filling with tears as she caught sight of the simple silver chain and the pendant that read #1 Mom.

"Thank you, Eli. It's perfect." She hugged him tight, then

reached around to take off her white-gold and diamond necklace.

"Are you going to wear the necklace *I* bought you?" Eli looked shocked, and Maggie nodded.

"Of course. Today is my first day of being your mother. I want everyone to know it."

"I guess maybe that means I can call you Mom now."

"I guess it does." She put the silver necklace on, then took Eli's hand. "Ready?"

"If you are."

They stepped out of the room together, following Jenna and Edith through the corridor, the sound of organ music beckoning them on.

The sanctuary doors were closed as they approached, and two tuxedoed men swung them open. Jenna and Edith walked through first. Kane's father followed.

And then it was Maggie and Eli's turn.

Her heart raced as she heard the swelling strains of the bridal march, and for a moment Maggie didn't think she could move.

This was it.

She was going to marry the man of her dreams, was going to finally have the family she'd always wanted.

Please, God, don't let me mess this up.

Eli squeezed her hand and looked up into her face. "It's going to be okay, Mom. *We're* going to be okay."

She stepped into the sanctuary. Kane stood at the end of the aisle, dashing and handsome in his tuxedo, his smile filling up the emptiness that had made her doubt and worry.

Edith was right.

Eli was right.

This was right.

She took a deep breath and placed her hand in Kane's,

felt his warmth and strength seep in, chasing away the nerves, leaving nothing but love.

"You're stunning." His knuckles brushed her cheek, his fingers leaving a trail of fire.

"So are you."

"Can boys be stunning?" Eli whispered, and Jenna let out a quiet laugh.

"Are you sure you want to marry into this crew?" Kane said with a smile, and Maggie squeezed his hand.

"They're my family."

"And *you* are the love of my life." He leaned down and pressed a gentle kiss to her lips.

"Hey, no kissing before the deal is sealed," someone said, and Maggie laughed, turning to face the pastor. Kane on her right. Eli on her left.

Her family.

There was nothing to fear, nothing to worry about.

There was simply joy, simply love, simply a thousand dreams finally coming true.

And it was *so* right.

* * * * *

Dear Reader,

Running Scared is a story about danger. It is a story about love. Perhaps more than all those things, it is a story about grace.

Maggie Tennyson grew up tough, and she's made a lot of mistakes because of it. Now a Christian, she's turned away from the hard-partying lifestyle and is trying to make a better life for herself. When she becomes embroiled in a missing child's case, everything she's worked for is threatened. If she's going to survive, Maggie must rely on private investigator Kane Dougherty to help her track down the man who nearly killed her three years ago. As she and Kane face danger, they must also face the past and learn that God's grace truly is sufficient for them.

I hope you enjoyed reading their story as much as I enjoyed writing it, and I hope that whatever your past has been, your future will be filled with the wonders of His mercy and grace.

God bless,

Shirlee McCoy

QUESTIONS FOR DISCUSSION

1. What is Maggie's biggest challenge as she tries to live her life for God?

2. Maggie has repented of her sin and is trying hard to move on. What is it that keeps her from fully accepting that she is forgiven?

3. Kane has prayed for a miracle for five years and finally gets it. How does the reality of it measure up to the dream?

4. How does Kane feel during the years that he's waiting to be reunited with his son? What is it that he struggles with the most?

5. When Kane tells Maggie that she is family, how does she feel? Why?

6. What is it about Eli that reminds Maggie of herself? How does this affect her relationship with him?

7. Kane wants desperately to reconnect with his son, but Eli is nothing like the child he remembers. How does he reconcile the child he has with the child he lost?

8. Why is Maggie hesitant to tell Kane about her past? What is she afraid will happen when she does?

9. How does she feel when she realizes that Kane knows the truth about who she once was?

10. What do you think makes Kane able to accept Maggie's past?

11. As Christians, what should our response be to those who are truly repentant?

12. Maggie never had a good example in her life of what it means to love and be loved. Yet, in the end, she is willing to mother Eli. What is it that gives her the courage to believe that she can be the mother he needs?

13. Although Maggie is a young Christian, she understands an important truth about repentances. She knows that it does not simply mean saying she is sorry, but also involves completely turning her life around. Has she accomplished this?

14. What could you achieve if you didn't let past mistakes keep you from moving forward?

Love Inspired
SUSPENSE

TITLES AVAILABLE NEXT MONTH

Available August 10, 2010

LARGER-PRINT BOOKS!

**GET 2 FREE
LARGER-PRINT NOVELS
PLUS 2 FREE
MYSTERY GIFTS**

Love Inspired®
SUSPENSE
RIVETING INSPIRATIONAL ROMANCE

Larger-print novels are now available...

*Five hunky Texas single fathers—five stories from
Cathy Gillen Thacker's* LONE STAR DADS *miniseries.
Here's an excerpt from the latest,* THE MOMMY PROPOSAL
from Harlequin American Romance.

"I hear you work miracles," Nate Hutchinson drawled. Brooke Mitchell had just stepped into his lavishly appointed office in downtown Fort Worth, Texas.

"Sometimes, I do." Brooke smiled and took the sexy financier's hand in hers, shook it briefly.

"Good." Nate looked her straight in the eye. "Because I'm in need of a home makeover—fast. The son of an old friend is coming to live with me."

She was still tingling from the feel of his warm palm. "Temporarily or permanently?"

"If all goes according to plan, I'll adopt Landry by summer's end."

Brooke had heard the founder of Nate Hutchinson Financial Services was eligible, wealthy and generous to a fault. She hadn't known he was in the market for a family, but she supposed she shouldn't be surprised. But Brooke had figured a man as successful and handsome as Nate would want one the old-fashioned way. *Not that this was any of her business...*

"So what's the child like?" she asked crisply, trying not to think how the marine-blue of Nate's dress shirt deepened the hue of his eyes.

"I don't know." Nate took a seat behind his massive antique mahogany desk. He relaxed against the smooth leather of the chair. "I've never met him."

"Yet you've invited this kid to live with you permanently?"

"It's complicated. But I'm sure it's going to be fine."

Obviously Nate Hutchinson knew as little about teenage

boys as he did about decorating. But that wasn't her problem. Finding a way to do the assignment without getting the least bit emotionally involved was.

Find out how a young boy brings Nate and Brooke
together in THE MOMMY PROPOSAL,
coming August 2010 from Harlequin American Romance.

Love Inspired
HISTORICAL
INSPIRATIONAL HISTORICAL ROMANCE

Bestselling author

JILLIAN HART

brings readers
a new heartwarming story in

Patchwork Bride

Meredith Worthington is returning to
Angel Falls, Montana, to follow her dream
of becoming a teacher. And perhaps get to know
Shane Connelly, the intriguing new wrangler on
her father's ranch. Shane can't resist her charm
even though she reminds him of everything he'd like
to forget. But will love have time to blossom before
she discovers the secret he's been hiding all along?

*Available in August
wherever books are sold.*

Steeple
Hill®
LIH82841

A soft shuffling